"You ha[...]
You migh[...]
hesitantly.

"Oh, yes, I have," he whispered. His large hands splayed across her lower back, and she felt them tremble. "I've known you forever. Your grandmother told me everything about you. I even know about the tiny mole you have right here."

His hand slid down and touched her gently, intimately, as if she weren't wearing any clothes. His thumb circled the small, secret dark spot, and she drew a weak breath.

"No," she whispered.

"Yes." He lowered his head. "I love the way you look when you wake up, all mussed and expectant. I have to kiss you," he said in a raspy voice.

She swayed against him, as a flower turns toward the sun. And his lips came down on hers. He'd cast a spell over her, and she couldn't escape the breathless wonder of his enchantment. . . .

WHAT ARE *LOVESWEPT* ROMANCES?

They are stories of true romance and touching emotion. We believe those two very important ingredients are constants in our highly sensual and very believable stories in the *LOVESWEPT* line. Our goal is to give you, the reader, stories of consistently high quality that may sometimes make you laugh, sometimes make you cry, but are always fresh and creative and contain many delightful surprises within their pages.

Most romance fans read an enormous number of books. Those they truly love, they keep. Others may be traded with friends and soon forgotten. We hope that each *LOVESWEPT* romance will be a treasure—a "keeper." We will always try to publish

LOVE STORIES YOU'LL NEVER FORGET
BY AUTHORS YOU'LL ALWAYS REMEMBER

The Editors

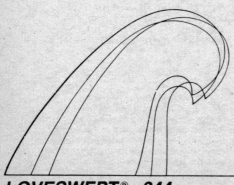

LOVESWEPT® • 344

Sandra Chastain
Joker's Wild

 BANTAM BOOKS
NEW YORK • TORONTO • LONDON • SYDNEY • AUCKLAND

JOKER'S WILD

A Bantam Book / August 1989

If you would be interested in receiving protective vinyl
covers for your Loveswept books, please write to this address
for information:

Loveswept
Bantam Books
P.O. Box 985
Hicksville, NY 11802

ISBN 0-553-21992-8

PRINTED IN THE UNITED STATES OF AMERICA

O   0 9 8 7 6 5 4 3 2 1

For Irene

One

Allison Josey slammed the door of her beloved red MG with her good knee, fitted her crutches under her arms, and awkwardly made her way across the courtyard into her grandmother's garden. She'd driven for almost three days to get there, and she was determined to sit in the gazebo.

The scent of freshly mown grass was sweet and familiar. But the sight of the latticework structure wasn't. It had become weathered over the years and was no longer white. By the time she reached the gazebo, where she'd spent so many happy hours as a child, her knee was throbbing with pain, and there was an ache in her throat. The place wasn't at all as she'd remembered it.

Propping her crutches against the banister, she pulled herself determinedly up the steps. She'd made it—on her own. It didn't matter that the paint was flaking and peeling. She was finally there. "Home," she whispered, just as her bad knee gave way, and she stumbled inside.

Two arms caught her as she fell and lifted her against a bare, rock-hard chest that cushioned her face with soft downy hair and smelled like the woods after a rain. She felt the slow, steady beat of a person's heart beneath her cheek.

"Hold on there, darling, you've reached the castle. I'll pull up the drawbridge and stave off the attack."

"Oh! I beg your pardon." Allison's voice was a choked sputter as she tried to settle her whirling senses back to normal. She was being held by a titian-haired, bearded giant of a man wearing faded jeans and a half-buttoned green plaid shirt.

"You never have to beg, Beauty."

"I didn't mean to . . . I mean I didn't see you or I wouldn't have . . ." Unwelcome tears of frustration welled up in her eyes.

"It's all right. With a rainstorm of salty tears blinding your vision, you couldn't be expected to see anything."

"I don't cry," she protested wearily. "I'm just exhausted."

"Don't worry, darling"—his teasing dropped off and his voice became soft—"you're in Joker's territory now. I'll protect you."

Caught by the tenderness in his voice, Allison tilted her head and looked up, straight into the biggest, deepest gray eyes she'd ever seen. Little laugh lines fanned out from their corners as his eyes flashed in merriment. In spite of their deep, smoky color, they seemed perfectly matched to the face of the burly, bronze-colored giant.

Thick auburn hair curled damply about the man's forehead, and a darker brick-colored beard covered his face and upper lip. She had the absurd feeling that she'd stumbled into a time warp and was looking at Eric the Red standing on the bow of a Viking ship.

For the longest time they stood, not speaking, simply gazing at each other. She knew she ought to pull away from his embrace, ought to remove her fingers from his massive chest. But all she could do was look up at him in bemusement. She had to be dreaming. There couldn't be a man in the gazebo in her grandmother's garden in Pretty Springs, Georgia, at eleven o'clock in the morning.

He nodded as if in reassurance. "You're Allison. Your grandmother said you'd come."

"Who are you?"

"I'm Joker."

"You can't be real. I must be more tired than I thought."

"Oh, yes, I'm real. I've been expecting you."

"You have?" She felt a bit light-headed. This couldn't be happening, she told herself. Her grandmother was in a nursing home. Why would a stranger named Joker be on the grounds? Yet the man's arms were solid and warm. She knew instinctively that he was the kind of man a woman could lean on, a man who feared nothing. For the first time in a long time she felt secure.

"But why?" she asked, feeling as if she were a child again, there in the gazebo with Gran, asking questions. Why are the stars so tiny? Why does the wind blow? She hadn't asked questions for quite a while. Trained athletes didn't ask questions. They followed instructions. And she had, until she'd checked herself out of the hospital and run away from all those instructions.

"Why?" The big man repeated softly, pushing back a stray tendril of midnight black hair that had curled across her cheek. He caught it between his fingers and rubbed it back and forth as if he were studying a priceless treasure.

"Never question fate, darling. Just accept what it sends. You need me, and I'm here." Reluctantly he tucked the strand of hair behind her ear and trailed his fingertips across her shoulder and down her back. He didn't know what was wrong, only that she needed him.

"No. What I need is to walk again, skate again. The doctors told me that I'll never skate again, and I must. Do you understand?"

"I understand, Allison Josey. For now, just lean on me."

She rested her weight on her good leg, allowing him to support her with his big arms and strong body. Gran had told him to expect her? That was all that she needed to hear—for now. He seemed to be part of home, the steady comfort she'd been drawn back to, and she looked up at him once more, a wistful expression on her face.

"All right," she agreed, too tired to put up a fight. "But I should know why, shouldn't I?"

"Because I'm here, and I need you too," he answered.

Joker felt he knew the dark-haired woman with the haunting eyes he held in his arms. She was the same graceful beauty whose photographs and news clippings papered the study wall in the main house. She'd fascinated him, captured his attention with her ethereal loveliness. For more than six months he'd taken the image of her to bed with him every night and had woken with her every morning. But this time she wasn't wearing a gossamer ice-skating costume or being held by a slender man in some dreamlike skating pose. She was in his arms—and she belonged there.

Allison Josey's appearance in the garden was no surprise to him. He'd already heard so much about her from her grandmother. He'd expected her, sooner or later. Now that she'd come, he had no intention of defying fate. The minute he'd seen the crutches he'd known that she'd come to him because she was bruised, hurt, in need of care. When she fell into his arms, he knew it was up to him to nourish her and make her bloom.

There was a hush in the garden, as though they'd slipped into a secret place where no one else could go. The sun was warm, the smell of honeysuckle sweet. Allison looked up at him with soulful eyes that drew him and held him imprisoned by the pain reflected there.

And then he kissed her.

As he lowered his head, Allison's eyes widened in surprise. She couldn't believe that his lips were touching hers. Her body seemed to sigh, rippling pleasantly as she sagged against him.

Suddenly, she could feel a fluttering inside her like a butterfly's wings, as the floor of the gazebo seemed to float beneath her feet. For a moment she wasn't sure she was breathing. The sun seemed to brighten, shooting a shimmering curtain of warmth through the vine-wrapped roof. She swayed against him, her fingers tangling in the hair on his chest. She returned his kiss as naturally as if she'd expected it, as if she'd known he'd be waiting there—for her.

When he finally lifted his head, she stumbled backward and tried to speak. "I . . . I don't understand. This can't be happening. I must be daydreaming," she whispered.

"Daydreams are mirrors of the soul's desire. That's what your grandmother told me."

"Gran?" Yes, she thought, that sounded like something her grandmother would say. Allison gazed at him for a moment as she tried to collect her thoughts.

"Oh, yes. She told me all about you, Allison Josey. You'll celebrate your twenty-seventh birthday in December. You like fried chicken. You're stubborn. Red is your favorite color, and you've been waiting for me. I think that just about covers it."

His voice was low as he leaned closer. She could feel the warmth of his breath against her cheek. His beard was touching her forehead.

"Eric the Red?" she whispered under her breath. She trembled and pushed against him, reality nudging into the serenity of the moment. "I don't understand. This can't be happening. Let me go. Please!"

"Don't be afraid, Beauty," he said. "Sit here on the banister. I'll release you—for now. But we've touched, and I'm part of you. You can never again erase the me from you."

The stranger stepped away, and Allison's heart pounded even harder. She'd been right. He was large, not heavy but tall and muscled, a man who worked with his hands and his body. This was no gym-shaped hunk. This was a man who was a part of the earth, a part of the universe, a part of her now, and she yearned to reach out and touch him again.

"Listen, I'm a little spacey from driving for the last five hours without stopping." She jutted her chin forward and continued more formally, "I wasn't expecting anyone to be here. I don't normally fall into strange men's arms."

"Strange? No. Once you kissed me, I stopped being a stranger."

As the absurdity of the situation hit her, Allison gathered her scattered senses and said, "When I kissed you? Stop kidding around, mister. I'm too exhausted to deal with this right now."

He didn't answer her. He just stood inches away from her as though he were waiting for her to come back into his arms. Every nerve ending in her body strained toward the security of those arms. She began to wonder if she might be having an out-of-body experience.

"I understand, Beauty. I know you're tired."

"Beauty? All right, why do you keep calling me that? Is this fairy tale time? Are you acting out some kind of Beauty and the Beast fantasy?"

"No, darling," he said gently, a patient smile on his face. "I'm just a man, a simple gardener. I make things grow. And if you'll let me, I'll bring a bloom back to your cheeks and teach you about a sweet and loving life."

"Honestly now," she protested weakly, "no more fun and games. I don't know who you are or what you're doing here, but this is my home. Or it was my home until I moved to . . . that doesn't matter. I've been driving for a long time. I'm totally wiped out, and I don't think I can stay awake much longer. Please, let me go!"

"I'm not holding you, my Beauty. You're free to go whenever you like. But I'm here. All you have to do is need me, and I'll come to you."

He really wasn't touching her, Allison realized. His nearness was an illusion that lingered. She still felt him, felt the strength of his arms and the warmth of his touch. Then the feeling was gone, and she shivered as he lifted her hand, touching her palm to his lips before moving away.

Allison blinked once and then rubbed her eyes in disbelief. She had to be hallucinating. She closed her eyes and breathed deeply. When she opened them again, she was alone. She wasn't sure how much had been real and how much she'd imagined.

It must have been the aftereffects of the painful knee injury that had colored her mind and made her see what she'd needed to see. She'd read about women who wanted a child so badly that they gained weight, suffered morning sickness, and even produced milk when they weren't even pregnant. Did she want a tender, caring lover so much that she'd conjured one up? No! She was in the gazebo in her grand-mother's garden. She'd come home to get away from the world and let herself heal. Only . . . she hadn't taken any pain pills since she'd left the hospital. Whatever had happened hadn't been induced by her medication.

In the distance she heard a lawn mower start up.

The limbs of the great oak trees hung still and graceful in the garden around the gazebo. A quick little breeze caught the leaves and moved them, stirring the quiet peacefulness with secretive whispers. Sounds of the garden sifted through her confusion, and she took a deep, sweet-scented breath.

This was Pretty Springs, Georgia. This was home. After fourteen years she was back where she'd started. She could wash her face, take off her shoes, and eat brownies and pancakes and fried chicken forever. She'd never be half of the team of Josey and Saville again. She'd never be married to Mark Saville. The couple whose faces had been plastered across the covers of every gossip magazine from the moment they'd won the Olympic gold medal five years ago was no more. Mark had found someone else.

For almost six months she'd been plain old Allison Janette Josey, who couldn't manage on dry land any better than she could skate on ice. She swung around into the doorway, picked up her crutches, and hobbled down the steps toward the house.

"Damned knee! Damned doctors. I'll show them all. I will skate again!"

In the distance the auburn-haired man watched the delicate woman move awkwardly and stop every few steps to rest and look around as if she were taking her bearings. She seemed to be breathing in the scents and feel of home. As if she were some music-box ballerina, she raised her head defiantly and slowly turned around, her body language indicating a change in her attitude from defeat to a tentative acceptance. A half smile washed across her face, and she opened her arms as if she were a butterfly emerging from a cocoon.

Joker nodded. He understood her feelings about this place. It had been while he'd been landscaping the Pretty Springs Golf and Tennis Retirement Community nearby that he'd found Elysium and fallen in love with it—and the gentle elderly lady who owned it. His brothers understood why he preferred renting the carriage house on the grounds of Elysium to living in one of the condos they were building. They'd learned about saving precious things. They'd saved the healing mineral springs at the golf and tennis housing community by incorporating the Sports Medicine Rehabilitation Center into the project.

The first day he'd driven by the wisteria-covered stone entranceway to the estate, he'd been intrigued. Without any hesitation he'd driven down the lane lined with deep red crape myrtle trees and had seen the lovely old house and gardens falling into disrepair. When Lenice Josey welcomed him inside, he'd known that he wanted to stay. She quickly became the grandmother he'd never had. And he'd become her fierce protector. She'd rented him the carriage house, and he'd moved in.

And then he'd seen the photos of Allison. From that moment he'd been captured by something more than the house, by a need he couldn't identify, an obsession for the hauntingly beautiful Allison on the silver skates. He couldn't have left, even if Lenice Josey hadn't welcomed him like a grandson.

It wasn't until he'd found Mrs. Josey crumpled on the kitchen floor and had taken her to the hospital that he'd discovered the perilous state of her finances. Only her concern for her granddaughter had kept her from selling out and moving into a retirement home long ago. But it was clear that Allison had her own life, a life outside of Pretty Springs. And Mrs. Josey knew that Allison's love for Elysium wasn't for the place itself but for her. Then, Lenice had fallen ill, and she'd had no choice.

As long as she owned the estate she was unable to qualify for the extended medical assistance she needed. Mrs. Josey had to sell to pay off the hospital and supplement her own meager income. Whatever was left over would then go to Allison later. But she'd made everyone involved promise that Allison wouldn't be told—until Mrs. Josey could tell her herself.

Joker couldn't allow a stranger to tear down the estate or turn it into co-ops or condos. He'd offered to buy the place, and she'd agreed, knowing that the chances of Allison ever living there again were slim. At least if Joker bought it, it wouldn't be swallowed up in new development.

At the time, Lenice Josey's doctor had notified Allison of her grandmother's fall, but Allison was scheduled to undergo the operation on her knee, and she couldn't come. Joker became Mrs. Josey's family. But he continued to live in the carriage house, even after the house became his. The house was meant for a family, and he'd been alone—until now.

The exterior needed to be painted, the roof leaked, and some of the windows had begun to rot away. But Joker couldn't bring himself to change anything. Now he knew why. He'd kept it just the way it was for the woman in the pictures. He just hadn't anticipated that she wouldn't know that the home she'd come back to wasn't hers any more.

The expression of defeat on Allison's face as she made her way to the gazebo had been no surprise to him. He'd been down the same lonely road, trying to find the sense of home he'd lost. Now he knew that he'd been walking toward her with every step he'd made.

Allison didn't need to be told yet about his arrangements with her grandmother. She hadn't been informed about their friendship or that his large monthly house payments were supplementing Miss Lenice's small income. He'd explain everything to Allison when the time was right. He wasn't sure why Allison had come home or what she needed, but he felt her pain as though it were his own. Learning that Elysium belonged to him now could set her recovery back even more.

Joker looked around the gazebo and felt the lingering aura of Allison's presence. He let out a cry of joy and gave an imaginary high five to the bright sunshine and whispering summer breeze.

Allison climbed the back steps and entered the kitchen as though she'd been thrown back in time. She was a schoolgirl again, hurrying home to share her day with Gran, calling out as soon as she entered the kitchen. The woman behind the sink would smile, hold out her cheek for a kiss, and go on whipping potatoes with a large metal fork.

Allison would fling herself down in the chair at the table by the bay window overlooking the garden and enjoy whatever treat Gran had prepared, while she told her grandmother about her day. She hadn't known what it was like to have a best friend to play with after school. She'd had Gran, and Gran had been enough.

Allison glanced around the kitchen. It was exactly the same—the faded marble countertops, the glass-fronted cabinets filled with the gold-colored Depression glass plates and glasses that Gran had received as wedding presents. She'd eaten on those dishes every day for thirteen years, until she'd left to train for the Olympics.

The ice-skating rink had been built on a vacant lot near her house when she was eight years old. The rink had quickly taken the place of the friends she'd never had. Skating had been a wonderful escape for her. It had allowed her to express herself and had hidden the uncertainty she'd felt as an adolescent. The only success she'd ever experienced in her life had been while on the ice.

Allison ran her fingers over the marble countertop, feeling the smooth, cool finish. The house was quiet, and she shivered as the memories came crashing over her.

When she was thirteen Allison had been selected to go to the Olympics training school in Colorado. She'd been too young to understand the sacrifices Gran had made to pay her fees. She'd missed Gran, but for the first time in her life she'd had a chance to be special. And she'd never really come home again, except for brief visits.

Then she'd met Mark, and he'd become the most important person in her life. Now Mark was gone, Lenice Josey was in a nursing home, and the house was still and empty.

Allison looked around.

Tired . . . so tired of having to put on a stoic face before the world. She groaned out loud. She'd been so sure that she could do this alone. Before she'd always been dependent on somebody. First there had been Gran, then her coaches and trainers, then Mark, and finally her doctors. She'd been to the mountaintop and had come crashing down. Now it was up to her. No more dependency. No more living on her pride or hiding her feelings or her past.

Allison Josey had checked herself out of the hospital and had come home. She'd learned to skate while living in this house. Now, one way or another, she'd learn to walk again. She gritted her teeth and climbed the stairs, grimacing with every step.

She pushed open the door to her bedroom, flexing her arms and shoulders, which were strained from using the crutches. She glanced around and felt a great lump tighten her throat. Gran had kept the room just as Allison had left it. The cabbage-rose print spread and the pink sheets were on the bed. Her stuffed animals still lined the bookshelves on the wall, and the picture of her receiving her first skating trophy leaned against the mirror on her dressing table. She dropped her crutches and lay back across the bed, absorbing the feeling of home.

The presence of the man in the gazebo should have disturbed her, but it didn't. There'd never been a man in their house before, but he seemed to belong there. She'd have to talk to Gran about him as soon as she'd rested for a while. She closed her eyes, remembering his gentle kiss. The memory was a soothing balm to her frazzled nerves.

So weary . . . Allison was asleep seconds before the screen door of the porch below swung open. She didn't hear the steps of the big bearded man as he deposited her suitcases inside the bedroom and stood over her, watching the faint up-and-down movement of her chest as she slept.

"So fragile," he whispered, and forced away the overpowering urge he felt to cradle her in his arms. His heart ached for her. She was a wildflower, a rare wildflower hiding in a dark place away from the sun. He'd protect her—somehow.

Two

Fried chicken. Gran was frying chicken.

Allison opened her eyes. The late afternoon sun made fingers of wavy lavender light across the pale pink carpet in her bedroom. No, she wasn't dreaming. She was in her room, and she definitely smelled chicken frying.

Allison had craved fried chicken for days before she'd left the hospital. She'd been tired of struggling, tired of hurting. When the doctors admitted that her surgery had been only partially successful and that their plans for a second operation promised no guarantees for further improvement, she gave in to her longing and headed south. She'd decided it was time to go home and start over again.

With a groan Allison forced herself up. Reaching for her crutches she dislodged one from the foot of her bed, and it clattered to the floor. The noise had hardly died down when she heard the unmistakable thud of footsteps on the stairs.

"Who's there?"

"Just me, Beauty. Are you ready for dinner?"

It was the red giant, the earthy apparition who had kissed her in the gazebo. He was standing in her doorway wearing a pink gingham apron around his waist and a frosting of flour on his beard.

"Are you the cook too?"

"Yes, ma'am. I'm it—butcher, baker, and candlestick maker. And I do a mean Texas two-step on the side."

"Just as long as you understand that this little house is in Georgia, not Texas," she responded with a smile, "and there isn't a chicken on the place."

"Ah, shucks! Well, the rest of my talents may not have an outlet, but at least the lady has a sense of humor and the cook has a captive audience." With an elaborate bow, he scooped her into his arms and did a two-step routine out into the hallway to the stairs.

"Joker," she protested, "Wait a minute. I appreciate your kindness, but what are you doing here?"

"If you mean what am I doing in the house, I have kitchen privileges. If you mean what am I doing in the kitchen, I'm frying chicken."

He descended the steps to the kitchen.

Quirking one eyebrow, he grinned. "If you're asking what I'm doing at this precise moment, I could say that I'm exploring my baser instincts."

Joker stopped beside the breakfast table, slid his fingers up her rib cage, and shifted her weight seductively against him before placing her on the gray leather dinette chair.

"Stop taking advantage of my injury, nature boy, and tell me what you mean by kitchen privileges," Allison said in a breathy voice.

"Miss Lenice and I made an agreement. Until I get a new stove in the carriage house, I can use her—excuse me—your kitchen."

"So when will that be?"

"Look." He turned, pointing her grandmother's heavy mixing fork at her. "It's my turn. You answer my questions, and I'll answer yours. What are *you* doing here now? Miss Lenice's doctor said that you wouldn't complete your therapy for another six weeks."

His question brought her up short. What exactly was she doing there when her doctors and her therapist were in Boston? She didn't know. Looking for hope, for the courage to start again? Looking for a place where people didn't demand or make decisions for her?

"Well, I . . . I left early," she finally answered. "I needed to be near Gran." And she knew that was the only answer she had. She needed someone to say, whatever you want, Allison. She needed someone to believe in her as a person and love her unconditionally.

The bearded man wadded a corner of his apron in his hand, lifted the lid of the frying pan, and began to turn the chicken. "Maybe, but seeing you hobbling around, I think you need as much looking after as she does."

"I'm fine," she said with a catch in her voice. "Or I will be soon."

For the last three days she'd dreamed of nothing else but home. She knew that Gran was in the nursing home, and though she'd known it would be hard being there without her, she'd wanted the time to work out her problems—alone. But she wasn't alone. She had a knight in shining armor in her castle, her own private defender of the realm, whether she wanted him or not.

"It's obvious," he began, "that you're still unsteady on those crutches. Want to tell me about it?"

"No, I don't," she answered quietly. "I'm not accustomed to having a man wait on me. The men I know expect me to be the one who . . . well, let's just say that I'm not used to this kind of attention."

"You should be. I can't imagine a man not showering attention on you. He must have been a real jerk," Joker said, shaking his head. "Want me to hunt him down and feed him to the crocs?"

"Mark isn't—I mean, how'd you—" She bit back the question. Why was she protecting him? Mark, the favorite of the press. When she couldn't skate anymore, their breakup had made the front page of all the tabloids. He'd said it was temporary. Only she had known that the arrangement was permanent. Mark had loved her, but he'd loved skating more. And she'd lost him. She wasn't ready to talk about Mark or the future—not yet. Instead, she said, "You never answered my question. Who are you, Joker, and why are you here in my house?"

Joker continued to turn the chicken as his mind worked quickly. He didn't think that the time was right to break the news to Allison that the house she'd come home to was his. He had an idea that she was too proud to accept his charity, and he didn't want her to do something desperate. He'd just figure out a way to give her the time she needed to heal before he told her the truth.

Joker's brothers had always accused him of dancing to a different drummer. When Jack and King looked up, they saw the sky. Joker saw cornflower blue velvet with clouds like swirls of alabaster and magnolias. He never saw the bad if he could see the good. And if he couldn't find anything good, he just didn't see anything at all.

Joker had always thought that he and his sister Diamond were the most alike. She decorated the inside of peoples' worlds and he landscaped the outside. The real reason they enjoyed their work was because they made the world more beautiful.

The truth was that he'd never quite trusted reality. If he created a situation, it couldn't change or disappoint him. He never said anything that would hurt anybody else. Now he sensed that a little imagination could soften the blow for Allison.

A large crackle of grease spat from the pan and singed his hand. "Ouch! What I am is a gardener. Your grandmother needed help, and I needed a place to live." His answer was true enough.

"Gardener? What happened to Ollie?"

"Ollie? Don't know. I'd say it's been a while since he was here. Your grandmother has had a hard time finding help during the past few years."

"I can see. She should have told me."

"She didn't want to worry you. And since I needed a place to stay," he improvised as he cooked, conscious that she was beginning to lose that frantic look, "she let me rent the carriage house."

Joker removed the pieces of chicken from the pan and placed them on paper towels. "After Miss Lenice fell, we altered our agreement somewhat. I look after things for her in exchange for my keep. You know your grandmother. She thinks I'm such a sensible boy. She trusts me. And I promise, my gardening is almost as good as my cooking."

Boy? Allison smiled broadly. Her grandmother had a unique way of viewing the world. A boy? No, her grandmother's gardener might be many things, but a boy wasn't one of them. She sneaked a look at him.

His expression was serious. Unconsciously she watched his profile as he worked. She'd never met anyone like this man. There was something about him, an energy that seemed at war with his size and strength. Yet she could picture Gran and him sitting on the patio talking. Perhaps it was that kind of belonging that made Allison accept his presence in spite of her protests. He was the one who belonged in Gran's kitchen—not she. The thought made her sad. Somewhere along the way she'd lost the belonging.

"Almost ready," he said as he poured tea into familiar gold-colored glasses filled with ice.

Allison frowned and stretched her shoulders. She hadn't been so tired since she was thirteen and had skated in her first competition with Mark. She hadn't known then that he would become so important to her that she'd give up control of her life to please him.

"All right," she finally agreed. "I'll honor Gran's wishes. But I'm at home now, so we'll have to work out a schedule to share the kitchen." Allison took a big sip from the glass of iced tea he'd placed before her. "At least until I can talk to Gran about what we're going to do."

"Maybe you won't want to bother Miss Lenice about the details just yet, Allison. I mean, she's improved considerably, but she still has a way to go. Perhaps we could continue to share the kitchen for a while.

How do you like the fresh mint in your tea? It's straight out of my herb garden."

Allison swallowed the sweet liquid and watched as the red-haired man spooned peas and new potatoes onto two plates. To each he added a large golden chicken leg and a slice of cornbread dripping with butter, then placed them on the table.

"You mean you expect to traipse in and out of my house at will? You've got to be kidding."

"Well, maybe after your knee improves, we can take turns. I'll make breakfast, you make lunch, and we'll share the night duty."

"I don't eat breakfast, I can't cook, and how much better my leg will get is open to debate. All I'm interested in right now is sunshine, rest, and quiet."

"Fine. We can supply that. But breakfast is the most important meal of the day. I'll teach you to cook, and I think I can help with the leg too."

"Oh? Do you practice medicine along with your other duties?" she asked with a smile, thinking how much she liked his carefree attitude.

"I'm a whiz with injured plants, but I've never tried my skills on a person. Want to be my first patient?"

Allison shook her head, wishing for a moment that she was back in the gazebo. Nothing was as she'd expected it to be. Maybe she ought to go back and start over.

Joker leaned over the table and touched her face with his fingertips. "Don't worry. I promise you that what I have in mind for your leg is something very special. I'm a man of many talents, darling, and I'm going to teach you to appreciate every one of them."

There it was again, that tenderness. She'd thought

she'd imagined what had happened in the gazebo, but she'd been wrong. He'd kissed her, and she hadn't protested. Now he was barely touching her cheek, and she felt the promise of his protection as if he were telling her with words. What was there about this man that made her feel warm and secure with only a touch? What was wrong with her that she was allowing it?

"Don't. Please." She pulled herself out of his reach. "Tell me why you would want to live here in our carriage house."

"Because"—his gray eyes sparkled as he held her gaze—"the first time I saw this place, I knew it needed me. I'm going to bring it back to life as it was in the gay nineties when Pretty Springs was a famous resort."

"I don't think anybody can do that. In a few more years this whole area will be commercialized."

"Bite your tongue. Just imagine ladies in their soft pastel dresses and picture hats, strolling through the gardens arm in arm with dapper gentlemen wearing bowlers and carrying canes. Oh, darling, it will be grand."

"1890?" He'd caught her attention, and her question slipped out.

Joker sat down at the table and picked up his fork. "Did you know that Mark Twain came to dinner here with your great-grandfather? I'll bet he ate fried chicken too. What do you think?"

"I think you're crazy. How'd you find out all that?"

"Oh, this house is a treasure of history. Have you ever taken a good look in the library?" He took a big bite of chicken and began to chew lustily. "Dig in, darling. I made strawberry pie for dessert."

Allison allowed herself to be distracted by his exuberance. The food was good. For the first time in a long time she was hungry. Maybe it was due to Joker. Maybe it was due to being back at Elysium where she felt safe.

She took a few bites of the fried chicken and considered his question. "No, I guess I haven't taken a good look at the library. I never had much time for reading. Once I started skating, all my spare time was spent at the rink."

"How old were you?"

"Eight years old and scared silly. Besides that, I had three left feet."

"But you learned. You must have figured out how to conquer your fear. That's good."

"Yes, well, it wasn't easy." She brightened and gave him a half smile. "I guess I never did get over my fear, but I learned to live with it."

"What about friends?" Joker asked with a cautiousness he didn't understand.

"There weren't many. I didn't fit in. I always had to practice so early in the morning that I couldn't stay up very late at night. The only time I ever went to a school dance I fell asleep in a corner of the gym and woke up when they were turning out the lights."

"What, only one school dance? Well, that will be our second order-of-recovery business. I still have my Elton John records somewhere. How are you fixed for miniskirts?"

"Elton John? I skated to one of his songs in a local competition. That was when my instructor decided I was good enough and moved me off to Colorado to live with a real coach. After that I never had time for history or dances either."

"That's all right. We've got plenty of time. I'll teach you while you're getting rid of those crutches."

"If you're a betting man, Joker"—she allowed the pain and doubt to creep into her voice—"you could be bankrupt before you get started."

"Oh, I'm a betting man all right. But that's another story. I'll tell you about my gambling habits tomorrow after breakfast." Joker turned his attention to his food.

"I told you, I don't eat breakfast. I have to watch my weight. I have . . ." Her voice trailed off. "No, I don't have to—not any more. But I'm not having breakfast with you. I don't know you."

She wasn't sure that she wanted to know this man who seemed intent on becoming a part of her life. For too long somebody had been directing her, planning her every move. She wasn't sure how to go about it, but she had to decide what she was going to do, not this stranger, no matter how soothing his presence was.

"We can fix that." He formally extended his hand. "Allison Josey, meet Joker. Joker, this dark-haired beauty is Allison Josey, a very special lady who needs you more than she knows."

Allison felt his big warm hand cover hers and trembled at the instant glow she felt as they shook hands. He smiled. "Needs you?" She pulled her hand away and glanced down. "Why do you keep saying that?"

Joker watched as she listlessly pushed the food around her plate with her fork. The cornbread had disappeared, along with a few bites of chicken and some peas. He could see that she had no interest in the rest of her food.

"Because when I touch you, I can feel your pain. I don't expect you to understand what I'm saying, Allison. Just trust me. I'm going to be your friend. I know that you've been sick, that someone has hurt you, and that you've come home to get well."

Allison's head shot up. "How do you know that? Does my grandmother know what happened?" She couldn't keep the alarm from her voice. She'd meant to write to Gran and tell her the whole truth, but Gran had fallen and had ended up in the nursing home before she could. The stories about Mark's new partner had hit the gossip sheets while Allison was having her knee operated on, and by that time it was too late.

"No, don't worry, Beauty, it's all right. Miss Lenice knows that you had surgery, that's all. I just get special feelings sometimes. I can sense certain things."

"And that makes you a friend?"

"Not yet, but we'll work on it."

His words didn't seem strange. There was an atmosphere of well-being in the room that seemed at odds with the uncertainty she ought to be feeling. She felt as if she were acting out a fantasy, being there in her grandmother's kitchen, calmly eating fried chicken with a red-haired giant with a beard.

"It's been a very long time since I've had a friend who didn't want something from me. Maybe I'd like to believe you, Joker, more than you know. But I'm not sure that I know how to trust anybody. I'm not even sure what I expected to accomplish by coming home."

"Sometimes we don't understand why things happen," Joker said seriously. "I just knew the moment I came to this house that this was where I belonged. I need this place, and you need me. What say we help each other? Deal?" He took her hand again and squeezed it gently.

"Joker, I'm sure my grandmother is immensely fond of you, but I really came here to . . . be alone to make decisions that only I can make. I don't know if I can do that if you're constantly around. You seem to be able to get inside my mind and that bothers me."

"I don't want you to be afraid of me, Beauty. I only want you to be well." He stroked the palm of her hand with his thumb, feeling her tension begin to disappear. He hadn't meant to make her uneasy. He hadn't meant to touch her. But she seemed to need him.

"All right," she finally agreed, sliding her fingers from his grip. "If Gran trusted you, so will I, for now—if you'll confine your work to the grounds. It's getting late, and I'm very tired. Just leave the dishes, and I'll do them tomorrow."

She struggled to her feet, looked helplessly around, and turned back to the man sitting on the other side of the table. "Would you please bring me my crutches? I'm afraid I can't get far without them."

"No problem, Beauty, I'll take you up. I need to close the other bedroom doors."

"Why?"

Joker swung her up into his arms and started up the stairs. "So that the attic fan will pull cool air through your bedroom windows."

"That's not what I meant. I mean, why do you insist on carrying me?"

"You're too tired to be steady on those crutches

tonight. If you have to go some place during the next few days, I'll carry you—until you can walk there on your own."

"You'll do no such thing. You're not an orderly or my houseboy. I appreciate your kindness, but I need to practice being on my own."

"And I told you that we're going to be friends, Allison Josey. A friend never turns his back on another friend. And I have a very strong back. I won't let you fall."

He was doing it again, creating a kind of still, secret calm with his touch. He made her feel warm and peaceful at the same time her senses were reeling. She'd felt this same sort of frozen excitement before, just before she stepped onto the ice at a skating competition.

"Did my grandmother truly give you permission to stay in the carriage house?" Allison was forced to put her arms around his neck. His beard brushed her cheek, and his muscles quivered beneath her fingertips.

Joker felt how thin she was, and his concern grew. Her fighting spirit was still strong, but she might be physically incapable of coping with being alone. Her breast brushed against his elbow, and she jerked away. She wasn't as unaware of him as she pretended. He saw her studying his face and he smiled.

"Yes, ma'am. Miss Lenice took me in, she did, as I expect she'll tell you tomorrow. I'll take you for a visit."

"Visit? Oh, no. I can't go out yet. I'll call her. I don't want her . . . anyone to see me on crutches."

He reached her bedroom door, walked straight through to the bathroom, deposited Allison on the closed toilet seat, and turned on the water in the tub.

"You should take a hot bath and soak a while. I'll bring you a nightgown."

Allison stood quickly, groaned, and sank back to her seat, grimacing. "Please, Joker, go away, I'll manage on my own. I have to learn how—sooner or later."

"Later," he agreed and disappeared into the bedroom. In seconds he was back, holding a long cotton gown in a tiny pink rosebud pattern that had ruffles around the yoke and hem. "Tonight you have . . . a maid."

"A male maid?" Allison shook her head, taking the nightgown from his grasp. "I don't think so. For months I've had people dressing and undressing me, putting me to bed, and getting me up. I'll manage."

Joker saw the shadows under her eyes. She was exhausted, in pain, and uncertain of his motives, but she wasn't giving in. She had nowhere to turn, and he was overwhelming her. He hadn't meant to make her uncomfortable. The last thing he ever wanted to do was add to her pain. He took a step back, touched his fingertips to his lips, and blew her a kiss.

"All right. Good night, Beauty. I'll raise the draw-bridge and feed the crocs in the moat. Sleep well." He turned and pulled the door closed behind him, leaving a confused expression on the face of the woman of his fantasies.

"Good night," she whispered, catching a glimpse of the rosy-faced woman in the mirror before her. Suddenly she realized that the woman was herself. She was tired, but she looked . . . alive. Listening to

Joker's receding footsteps, she took off her clothes and stepped into the steamy water.

He was entirely too male. Nothing like the strong, graceful skaters she knew, this man was solidly in touch with the earth. Yet there was a mythical quality about him that reached out and found that tiny sliver of enchantment hidden deep inside her psyche. Beast? He wasn't a beast. He was just a man who was larger than life, who'd declared himself a part of hers.

Tomorrow she'd check with her grandmother about this red-haired Viking who'd appointed himself her protector—and friend.

"Oh, Allison," she heard him call out, "if you need me, just yell out the window. I'll hear you. And don't worry. You don't have to see anybody you don't want to. I know a back way to the nursing home."

Allison locked her bedroom door and leaned against it. She was going to bed even though there was a strange man on her property. Yet, curiously enough, she wasn't afraid. Joker. What a unique man he seemed to be, a man who seemed to care about her. Dare she believe him?

She'd believed Mark when he'd said he loved her. And he'd let her down. For him she'd skated when she shouldn't have, and now her career was over. Could she trust this man she barely knew? She shouldn't. But she did.

Allison unlocked her door and swung herself around to the window.

From the foot of the stairs, Joker heard the lock snap closed. Moments later he heard her unlock it again. He smiled and let himself out into the star-studded night. He stretched his taut muscles and breathed in the summer smells from the garden as he thought of Allison asleep upstairs in her brass bed with the pink print spread. His arms felt empty without her.

Standing in the courtyard, he could almost hear the night music, sweet and romantic, played by an imaginary string quartet in the gazebo. Yes, they would have walked there, those romantic couples from the past.

Through the window above the courtyard Allison watched the tall, muscular man take a deep bow and lift his hand. He began to waltz lithely around the garden, holding his imaginary partner gracefully in his arms. As he reached the steps leading up to the carriage house, he stopped, gave a second deep bow, and moved away into the darkness. Allison felt a pang of regret that the woman he'd held hadn't been she.

At the top of the stairs Joker paused. Like the town crier on his appointed rounds, he pealed out his evening report. "Ten o'clock and all's well. Or it will be," he whispered to the lady in the upstairs window.

He didn't turn on the lights as he walked through the moonlight into the bedroom. His quarters were old and comfortable. Only his bed was new. It had just been delivered. He looked down at it in the darkness. Massive, with four great oak posts and a square canopy over it, it was a bed made for sharing. There was a woman in the house he wanted to share it with. But she was wary of him, holding back, afraid to trust him. That was all right. Trust would come. He'd move slowly, as if he were taming a wild fawn or healing an injured plant. She'd come to him. He was convinced of it. Soon.

Through the open bedroom windows came the call of a night bird. Joker took off his clothes and lay on the bed. A wonderful, warm, peaceful silence settled over the estate. The moon went behind a cloud and the night folded itself around him.

The woman was beautiful. He rubbed his calloused hand across his beard. Fairy tale time? Maybe she was more right than she knew. "What we have here," he whispered out loud, "are Beauty and the Beast." And if he remembered the story correctly, she'd come just at the appointed time. So what if the tale had taken a different direction in real life? So what if the person in need was the Beauty and not the Beast? There was nothing wrong with taking a little literary license, he decided, and closed his eyes.

Three

The next morning Allison found her crutches propped against the table by her bed. She glanced around and spotted the suitcase she'd packed so hastily. It had been placed by her closet door. Pulling herself upright, she hobbled to the closet and opened the door. All her clothes were hanging neatly inside.

The work of the jolly red giant, no doubt, she thought. What was she going to do with the man? She smiled and slid her nightgown over one shoulder at a time until it floated to the floor. After so many knee injuries, she'd given up wearing slacks, opting instead for loose-fitting skirts and long-waisted dresses that were easy to put on and take off. Choosing a soft T-shirt dress of deep blue, she pulled it over her head, thrust one crutch under her arm, gritted her teeth, and headed barefoot for the kitchen.

At the base of the stairs she paused, waiting for the spasms of pain to subside. Bright sunshine filtered through the bay window overlooking the garden. Warming on the stove was a dented aluminum pot of freshly perked coffee. There was a slice of melon on a small plate in the refrigerator. Breakfast had been prepared by her cook, whether she wanted it or not.

Allison filled a coffee cup with the aromatic dark liquid, drank it quickly, and filled the cup again. Her gentle giant seemed to have vanished. By taking small steps, she was able to carry her cup, push open the sliding glass door that led to the old brick patio, and step outside. The morning sun was bright, the outside bricks pleasantly warm under her bare feet.

Leaning heavily against the backs of the wicker patio furniture, she swung her body around until she could sit on the chaise lounge. By then she was trembling with exhaustion. She lifted her bad leg, stretched out on the faded cotton cushions, and closed her eyes.

Years of rigid training had conditioned her body, but her muscle tone had deteriorated during the months she'd spent in and out of the hospital. Despite physical therapy, even a small amount of movement was exhausting. For more than an hour she simply lay there, soaking up the sun and napping, knowing that she ought to make some effort to replace the medication she had foolishly thrown away. The muscle spasms from her trip down the stairs earlier had proven to her that she wasn't ready to do without medication yet. But the sun was warm; the garden was peaceful. Except for the absence of her grandmother, Allison knew she'd made the right decision by leaving the hospital.

An area between the house and the gazebo had

been cleared, she noticed. Beyond that the famous Josey gardens had grown into a riot of tangled vines. The rose garden was almost totally choked by the deadly but sweet-smelling honeysuckle.

Allison felt a pang of guilt sweep over her as she realized the burden her grandmother must have faced. Everything had become too much for Gran, yet she'd never complained. Allison's last two visits home had been during the winter, and she hadn't realized the neglect. Shabby now, the great house was no longer the showplace of Pretty Springs. But it was home, and she understood Joker's attraction to the place.

She should have taken more interest in the place before her grandmother had fallen and been moved to a nursing home. Now everything was different. How on earth was she going to be able to stretch her funds to cover her own expenses and help pay for the repairs needed to keep the property?

There had been insurance to cover most of her hospital bills, but she wished she'd saved more of her earnings. She'd put money into her account, but there was always someplace new that Mark wanted to go or something he needed, and she'd never refused him anything. Once she'd checked herself out of the hospital, her only thought had been to come home. She had never considered the possibility that her home would be changed.

For now she wouldn't worry. It was enough to lie in the sun without pain. She didn't want to move. Even the roar of machinery in the distance didn't rouse her. Street traffic was so much a part of the pattern of her everyday life in the city that she never heard the motorcycle that sputtered to a stop behind the house.

"Wake up, my sleeping beauty. Your chariot awaits."

Allison's eyes opened drowsily. He was back; Eric the Red was kneeling beside her. But this morning he was wearing sharply creased khaki trousers and a Hawaiian print shirt. His beard had been neatly trimmed, and he'd gotten a haircut.

"You've cut your hair," she said. "You look like one of the Beach Boys. Do you sing, along with your other talents?"

"Me? Ha! Woman, my singing would scare buzzards. Come on, up with you. We have places to go and people to see. Where are your shoes?"

"They're upstairs, but I'm not going anywhere."

"Yes, you are. You're going to see your grandmother," he said quietly, and left the patio.

Before she could protest, he was back, sitting on the end of the wicker lounge, fitting her feet gently into a pair of soft leather loafers.

"Gran? I don't know. I'm scared, Joker. Gran doesn't know how bad my knee is, and I don't want her to worry."

"You think not seeing her will keep her from worrying?"

"You're right, and I'll go, but not today. I told you yesterday that I don't want to see anybody yet. I'm a mess."

Ignoring her protests, Joker handed Allison a lipstick and pulled a hairbrush from his back pocket. "I brought these from your dressing table."

Joker took the hairbrush and began to pull it through Allison's dark, silken tresses. He'd never brushed a woman's hair before, not since his sister

Diamond was very small. Though Allison held herself like the great stone sphinx, he found the action curiously gratifying.

"In your pictures your hair is always pinned up in a little knot. I didn't know it would be so long."

"Look, Joker, I know you think you're helping me. But I'd rather you didn't. I need to look after myself."

"Perfect!" he announced. "Now you can add hair-dressing to my list of talents." He lifted her and strode across the patio and around the house. He hitched up the hem of her T-shirt dress and deposited her on the back of the seat of a shiny red motorcycle. "Will this hurt your knee?"

"I'll manage," she said stiffly, knowing that it would be sheer torture.

"I'm sorry. We could drive your car, but I don't think I can squeeze into it, and my van is in the shop. We'll use it next time." He fastened a shiny red helmet over her head and a matching one over his own.

The man was impossible. Nothing stopped him. Once he'd declared an intention, he plowed full speed ahead. Here she was straddling a motorcycle, going for a visit she was scared silly to make, with a man she was growing to like more and more.

"What do you think, Beauty?"

"A red motorcycle? Why not?" She admitted with reluctant amusement, "I like a discreet man."

"Yes, well. I like color. It goes with my vibrant, exciting personality, don't you think?" He turned the key, and the machine roared to life. Allison's smile at the sight of the red bike had warmed his heart.

She held on for dear life as the machine lurched

forward. He definitely had a way of getting to her, she thought. "Eric the Red and a red bike? A perfect match," she commented dryly.

Joker didn't hear her. Her words were caught by the wind and flung away behind them as he maneuvered the machine around and drove down the long drive to the road. She tried to maintain distance between her thighs and his body, but the seat was amply filled by her companion, leaving little space for her slight frame.

As a skater she was more than used to two bodies moving together as one. But this sensation was disturbingly different. She couldn't tell whether it was the wave of pain radiating from her knee or the rough texture of his cotton trousers rubbing against the inside of her legs that set off the quivers in her lower body. The woodsy smell of his cologne whipped past her face and caught in the helmet she was wearing. And the feel of her breasts pressing against his back conjured up intimate forbidden fantasies that made her heart beat so fast that she was certain he could feel it through his shirt.

Allison forced her attention to the new buildings along the roadside. It's a matter of willpower, she told herself. If she didn't think about the pain, it wouldn't be there.

Gone were the big two-story houses that used to line the street across from the railroad. They'd been replaced by a bank, a new fire station, and an automobile dealership. She realized with a pang of regret that old Pretty Springs was no more.

The old Allison Josey is no more either, she thought. But the changes in the town were progressive and counted for something. Allison was still in transition, and she had no idea how she would revitalize her life.

Joker turned the motorcycle abruptly at the sign that said PRETTY SPRINGS NURSING AND RETIREMENT HOME. He cut down a gravel service road, circled to the back of the stately structure with the huge wraparound veranda, and brought the cycle to a stop under a magnolia tree. Allison realized gratefully that he'd respected her wishes not to be seen.

Joker removed his helmet and Allison's.

"Now you behave yourself, Beauty," Joker cautioned. "Or I'll check you in and let you share a room with your grandmother."

"I wish you hadn't done this, Joker. I don't want to worry Gran."

"She knows that you'll come sometime, and she's missed you—very much. Now you put a smile on that face, and let her see that you're doing fine." Joker lifted Allison's chin and planted a quick kiss on her lips. "Okay?"

"Oh, all right." He was doing it again, convincing her with his touch to follow the direction he'd already determined for her. And she was agreeing without a fuss. "But how do you plan to explain why I can't walk?"

"I'll handle that if you'll promise me something. Don't get shook, no matter what you see. And you're right," he cautioned, "we don't want to let her know how bad your leg is. She thinks we're just sneaking you in so that you won't be mobbed by your fans."

Joker lifted her once more and stepped across a low rock wall into a private patio shielded from the world by a hedge on one side and a canvas awning on the other. He opened the sliding glass door, walked inside, and deposited Allison at the foot of a hospital bed covered with a plush satin comforter.

"Morning, Miss Lenice, here's our girl."

Lenice Josey opened her eyes, a bright smile spread halfway across a mouth drawn into a downward grimace at one corner. With one hand she pulled Allison to her and hugged her. "Good boy," she said slowly, trying to erase the hesitation from her speech. "Joker said you . . . here. Your leg?"

Allison could only nod as her face paled at the sight of her grandmother. She'd received the call about her grandmother's fall just before the operation on her knee. Afterward she hadn't been able to do more than keep in touch with Gran's doctor by phone. Obviously Gran hadn't wanted to worry her, so she hadn't let him tell Allison the whole truth. Now she knew; the drooping mouth and the slurred speech indicated the fall hadn't been just a fall—she'd had a stroke.

"It's fine. How are you, Gran?" Allison hugged the thin woman, pulled back, and looked at her grandmother as she continued to hold her hand. Lenice Josey had suddenly grown old, and Allison hadn't noticed the change until now. To Allison, Gran would always be beautiful. Though Allison realized the staff was taking good care of her, her illness showed in her face. But she was still Gran. Her hair was styled, and the soft pink robe she was wearing complimented her carefully manicured pale pink fingernails.

"Good . . . better . . . you?"

"Much better now that I'm home. But I miss having you there. When are they going to release you?"

A frown creased one side of Mrs. Josey's face.

"It better be soon," Joker interrupted, his hearty voice teasing the elderly woman as he moved up beside her bed. "I'm going to have to sit outside this door with a big stick. Kaylyn and Sandi—Kaylyn's the recreation director and Sandi's the therapist—say that all the single men in the joint are courting Miss Lenice."

"Ahh, Joker, you're such . . . such . . . a tease."

"Yes, that's one of my charms, darling. Now don't tell anybody, but as soon as we can get rid of the wardens, I thought I'd take you out for a midnight spin on my new bike."

"Oh . . . you . . . I'm an old lady."

"I always was a sucker for an older woman."

"Not . . . me. Take Allison."

There was a light knock on the door as it swung open. "Mrs. Josey, it's time to get ready for our trip to the springs. Oh, sorry. I didn't know you had company." The woman in the doorway was tall, very tall, Allison noted. She was an absolutely stunning, statuesque, very pregnant woman.

Joker put his hand on Allison's shoulder as if he'd known she wanted to bolt from the room. "Kaylyn, this is Allison, Mrs. Josey's granddaughter. She's come home for a while. Allison, my sister-in-law Kaylyn."

"Oh, how nice. I've heard so much about you. Tom Brolin, the editor of the *Gazette*," Kaylyn explained to Allison, "was saying just last night that between you and the Vandergriffs, Pretty Springs is really on the map."

"Yep," Joker agreed. "But that's about to change. I heard this morning that Elvis Presley was spotted over at the springs. You've heard that he isn't really dead, haven't you?"

"Joker, how do you do it? Everybody else brings fruit. You bring fantasies. By the way," Kaylyn whispered behind her hand, "King said to tell you that Harold is looking for you. He's talked to the committee and they've decided to—"

"Harold?" Joker interrupted. "He isn't coming here, is he?" He knew what Harold's committee had decided. As soon as he'd told Mrs. Josey that Allison was home, the word had spread. Harold had come up with the idea of having Allison take part in the grand opening of the Sports Medicine Center. That was the last thing she needed to hear at the moment.

"Possibly. He was asking where—"

"Oh no! I forgot that Allison and I have an errand to run," Joker said, lifting Allison in his arms and striding out the door. "Give Harold my best," he called over his shoulder in a rush.

"Where are you going?" Kaylyn asked, shaking her head at her brother-in-law's foolishness.

"To buy some chickens," Joker said seriously. "We're considering turning the estate into a chicken ranch. Allison likes fried chicken."

Allison waved helplessly at her grandmother. Raise chickens? From the merriment in Gran's eyes it was obvious that she understood the man whooshing her out the door. Allison wished she did.

"What was that all about?" Allison asked as Joker fastened the strap of her helmet beneath her chin. She could have fastened it herself, but there was something soothing about feeling his hands softly touching her neck and chin. The feeling in her stomach as he straddled the machine and slid back against her was anything but soothing.

"What do you mean?" Joker yelled as he started up the motorcycle.

"Why did we fly out of there like we were about to be caught by the posse?" she asked when they stopped at a light.

"We were. You heard her say that Harold was looking for me."

"So? Who's Harold?"

"Harold is running for mayor, and you know how those politicians are, always campaigning."

By the time he'd parked the bike, Allison's leg was throbbing from the awkward position she'd had to hold her leg in while riding. All she had to do was continue her therapy, they'd told her, and she'd be able to walk. Walk? Maybe. Conquer her pain? No. Skate again? Never. The pain she could live with, but never skating again was something she refused to accept.

"Thank you," she managed to say, grateful for Joker's assistance this time. She couldn't have walked back to the house even if she'd had her crutches. She gave in to her weakness and laid her head against him, closing her eyes and tightening her muscles in an attempt to stop the agony.

Through the foyer, up the stairs, and into her bedroom he strode. He placed her on the bed and removed her shoes. "Your leg is cramping. Where is your medicine?"

"I threw it out the window somewhere outside of Washington," she answered, wondering again what she had hoped to prove by that piece of stupidity.

"All right, then. We'll improvise," Joker announced, taking the hem of her skirt and lifting it.

"What are you doing?" Allison panicked, grabbing his hand.

"I'm going to massage that knee. Then I'm going to pack it with hot towels. Try to keep it still until we can get you over to soak in the mineral water at the springs. It's brought a major league pitcher back to form. We'll see what it can do for you."

Joker left the room and she could hear him moving around in the bathroom. The situation was getting out of hand. She'd come home to get away from the world, only to find out that her safe refuge had been invaded by a stubborn stranger who seemed intent on taking over her life. She had to put a stop to that—somehow. Allison felt a fresh wave of spasms rack her leg, and she held her breath until it passed.

If she could get to a phone, she'd call . . . who? And . . . and do what? Report that she wanted to evict a red-haired giant who rode a red motorcycle and made her body flush with desire every time he touched her? No! Since the accident she'd avoided the press. She certainly didn't want to call attention to herself now.

First there had been her injury, then the slap in the face Mark had given her by quickly replacing her with a younger, more beautiful Olympic champion —on the ice and in his bed.

It took the time she'd spent in the hospital away from Mark for her to recognize the hypnotic effect of his power. Every gesture, every loving word had been a calculated seduction. He used all women, just as he'd used her. Mark didn't love anybody but himself. Once she could no longer perform, he didn't need her any more. That was when she realized that Josey and Saville would never be a team again.

She didn't know why she hadn't seen through him. Even now she refused to believe that Mark hadn't cared about her in the beginning. They'd been so young and so in love, the darlings of the press. For fourteen years it had been she and Mark against the world. She'd loved the ice, the fame, and the man. They'd all become jumbled together in her mind. Now she had to separate them out, and she wasn't sure that she could.

"I'm not going to any springs. I don't care if every pitcher in the National Baseball League is developing a bionic arm there," she managed to spit out between the waves of pain. "Where in hell are my crutches?"

"They're downstairs, Beauty. But I don't think you're ready for them. I'll get you a wheelchair this afternoon."

"No! No more wheelchairs! I will walk downstairs and get the damn crutches myself!"

"When camels fly! I shouldn't have taken you on my bike. You probably weren't supposed to drive, and I don't think you're supposed to be walking either, are you? Does your doctor even know where you are?"

"No, and he's not going to," Allison said wearily, bringing herself to an upright position. "I've come through other injuries and skated again. And I'll skate after this one, too, no matter what those doctors think. They aren't going to operate on me again. I don't need them, or anyone else."

Throwing her leg over the side of the bed, she gritted her teeth and attempted to stand. The minute her leg supported her weight, stars exploded behind her eyes, and she cried out in pain as she collapsed on the floor.

Joker was beside her instantly, lifting her back to the bed. He folded a pillow and slid it under her bad knee, forcing her skirt up, exposing her leg. "Damn! The surgeons really did a job on you, didn't they?" He stared in disbelief at the scars on her swollen knee. "You look like a racehorse I once knew. They gave up on him too. But after a little of my special attention, he raced again and won. Let me see what I can do for you."

She didn't answer. By that time the pain was too great. She closed her eyes and choked off the low moan rising from the back of her throat. And then she felt his hands, warm and gentle against her knee. She flinched and tried to move away. He didn't hold her. He simply rested his hands over her, letting the strange heat of his touch permeate the skin. Moistening first one palm then the other with a thick soothing cream, he rubbed.

The pain didn't stop, but soon she began to sense a kind of shield between her and the hurt. She began to relax and let herself respond to his tender touch. Nerve endings absorbed the heat, seemed to lose their tension, and settled into a glow. She parted her lips in a sigh, feeling a kind of spiritual aura settle over her.

On and on his hands worked, first gently, then more surely. As the bunched-up muscles relaxed, he moved to the other leg. Beginning with the toes, he worked his big hands up the slender, muscular leg, kneading out little knots of tension until she fell asleep.

Joker leaned back and waited. He'd always known he had good hands. He'd gently put many a plant in the ground and had watched each one settle in and begin to grow. He'd never thought much about his special power until he'd tried his touch on the horse's knee and seen it heal. This was the first time he'd applied it to a person. And like the bruised plants he'd brought back to life, Allison's leg had responded. Good. She was sleeping. She needed to sleep. She needed to heal. She needed his touch.

Hers was no simple injury, and he didn't think it was the only thing that was causing her pain. She'd been hurt so badly that she'd withdrawn from the world and come home to hide like a wounded animal. She was so strong, yet fragile and beautiful. He could probably span her waist with both hands and have enough space left to reach up and touch the small round breasts outlined by the knit fabric of the dress.

He felt himself harden as he looked at her. He wanted her, a woman half out of her mind with pain, more than he'd ever wanted a woman before. He wanted to take her pain and suffer it for her. He wanted to put his arms around her and tell her that everything would be all right. Instead, he only allowed himself to touch his lips to hers, holding them there for a very long minute.

"What do you mean, Diamond will have to take over the Chattahoochee Complex landscaping job? Jack designs our projects, I build them, Diamond plans the interior, and you handle sales and landscaping. This is a family project, or have you forgotten?"

"Oh, I haven't forgotten," Joker answered as he followed his brother King into the newly finished permanent offices of Vandergriff Development, Inc. in the Pretty Springs Golf and Tennis Retirement Community.

"Then why?" King's expression spoke his incredulity as he sat down behind the desk and propped his dusty boots on its marble top.

"I've met someone. She's alone, and she needs me. I want to be there for her."

"Her? You're asking one of us to do your job so that you can be there for a woman?"

Joker moistened his lips and nodded. "This woman is very special, King. I care a great deal for her."

King ran his fingers through his thick golden hair and said in an affectionate tone, "I don't think that there's been a span of more than a month in your entire life during which you didn't think you were in love with somebody, beginning with your first baby-sitter. You must have been the only four-year-old in history who proposed."

Joker walked to the window and looked out over the neat tree-shaded houses that surrounded the golf course. He couldn't see the lizard-shaped rock that was as much a part of the sports complex as the mineral springs that bubbled to the surface and collected in the natural basin, but he was proud that they'd saved it. He knew that telling King he cared about a woman was opening himself up to the brotherly teasing that was an easy part of their successful relationship, both in business and as a family.

He hadn't thought this far ahead, but now he realized that he expected King to understand. After all, from the moment the Pretty Springs Golf and Tennis Retirement Community had started and King had met Kaylyn Smith, he'd been a changed man. Joker had watched in amusement as King fell in love and began to view the world through Kaylyn's sympathetic eyes. Whether the Vandergriffs believed in the healing properties of Kaylyn's mineral waters or not, King's falling in love had forced all of them to come up with a plan that would allow the local citizens to continue to use the springs.

"I'm serious this time, King, as serious as you were when Kaylyn chained you to Lizard Rock to keep us from destroying the springs. I helped you come up with a solution then. Now I need your help."

King put his feet under the desk and sat up straight, a serious expression replacing his amusement. "You mean it, don't you? Who is she?"

"Her name is Allison Josey."

"Josey? As in the Josey estate, that run-down old house and gardens that you're buying from the old lady in the nursing home?"

"Allison is her granddaughter, yes. She's an ice skater, was an ice skater. She won an Olympic gold medal in pairs skating. She's come home, and she's . . . well, she's been hurt."

"Hurt?" King groaned. "Not another one. I think you should have studied medicine, brother, instead of horticulture."

"I might have," Joker agreed wistfully, "if the dean of admissions in the school of medicine had taken an interest in me and put my feet to the fire the way Ellen did."

"Leave it to you to find a woman who would offer you free room and board for four years. As it turned out, horticulture was the perfect choice for you. And I suppose Ellen was good for you too, although I'll never understand your relationship with her."

"I resent that, King Vandergriff. I cared for Ellen, more than you'll ever know. She made me realize that I could be somebody. You may not believe it, but our arrangement was a fair exchange. If she hadn't died, I might have . . . Forget it." Joker's voice didn't hide the hurt he still felt about Ellen.

"Sorry, I didn't intend to open a can of worms, Joker. I wouldn't dream of insulting anyone. I'm glad that Ellen was Dean of the Department of Horticulture. Once she took you in, you settled down and graduated, and I thank her for that. But," King allowed a hint of amusement to color his voice, "one of these days I'm going to get to the bottom of those field trips to Vegas and every racetrack in the west."

"I'd never do anything illegal, King. Let's just say I have a kind of understanding about certain things, and I've always believed in sharing. Sharing, brother, as in one family member stepping in and helping another when he asks."

"All right. We'll manage. After all, you already have everything planned out and ordered. I'll get Diamond to oversee the project. I trust you'll be by now and again, for consultation purposes?"

"Sure. I'll check in with you every day. But, King, don't come to the estate—not yet."

"Oh, I wouldn't think of ruining your little interlude."

"Allison Josey is the most beautiful woman I've ever seen."

King was frowning. "Allison Josey. . . . That name sounds familiar. I can't remember the details, but it seems to me that there was some kind of publicity about her a few months ago. I remember seeing a picture on the cover of a magazine." His forehead was furrowed by a mass of lines as he struggled to remember.

"You could have," Joker agreed. "She was very special. The whole world loved her. After the Olympics, she performed with an ice show, until she was injured again. Now she's come back home. Because of her health, she wasn't told about her grandmother's stroke, and she doesn't know about my buying the house. I don't want her to know just yet."

King stood up, looked at his watch, and walked toward the door. "Well, bring her over to the springs and let her take the mineral baths with the nursing home patients. You sure won't run into any traffic jams getting inside."

"Interest not picking up?"

"Interest? What interest? If it weren't for the home owners who love the golf and tennis facilities, the sports medicine center would be a total loss so far."

"Give it time, bro. Word will get around. Just wait until after the grand opening."

"Too bad we can't get somebody like your girlfriend to pass the word, assuming the springs helped her."

"That was Harold's idea too. I don't want to use Allison, King. The kind of injury Allison has is different. We can't be sure that the springs can help restore the use of her leg." Joker followed his brother outside. "Besides, she's still very self-conscious. I'm going to bring her down at night so that she won't be seen."

"Well, it's your decision. But it's your pocketbook if we go bust." King looked at his watch again. Joker could appreciate King's impatience. He knew it was time for Kaylyn and the nursing home entourage to arrive for their free visits. King always tried to be there when the group arrived. If it were up to him, he'd spend every minute with the woman who was carrying his child.

King was the first of the brothers to marry, and his joy had made Joker take a long look at his Casanova approach to life. After he'd discovered the Josey estate and the study wall plastered with pictures of a hauntingly beautiful dark-eyed woman, Joker had been content to stay in one place for the first time in his life. He'd made arrangements to buy the estate without realizing that the woman would be a part of the dream, the woman who was waiting for him to teach her how to heal.

They left the office together. King turned toward the springs, and Joker jogged out the door and over to his motorcycle. He fastened the red helmet beneath his chin and began to grin. Red. The sales clerk hadn't smiled when he selected the smaller one, but when Joker took the large one and put it on his own head, the clerk had grunted in disbelief. Eric the Red, Allison had called him. Hell, why not? The helmet had made Allison smile and that smile had been worth it all.

"Hey, Joker!" Kaylyn called out as she drove by in the nursing home van filled with patients. "Love your helmet. Come to dinner Saturday night. I'm inviting a friend over for Jack. I'll ask someone for you, too, if you like."

A friend for Jack? Kaylyn never gave up. His lone-wolf brother probably wouldn't even show up, and if he did, it was doubtful that he'd unbend enough to learn the woman's name.

"Maybe," Joker answered. "I'll have to let you know. It depends on . . . well, it depends on the crocs in the moat."

Kaylyn looked startled, but didn't comment. Joker knew that she took his joking in stride just as she did everything else in life. She'd like Allison, and Allison would like Kaylyn if they ever had a chance to get to know each other. Jack? Well, he'd just have to find his own damsel in distress.

Joker revved the engine and the motorcycle roared out of the parking area. He waved to one of the country's most famous football players, who was leaving his house and walking toward the golf course. The housing community was almost filled with celebrities and ordinary people living side by side playing tennis and golf. The Sports Medicine Center would eventually bring in world-class athletes of every sport. They hadn't had a skater at the center yet. But they would have—soon. Allison Josey just didn't know it yet, and the world would never know. Joker would see to it that Allison's privacy was protected. He wouldn't let her be used. There had to be another answer for calling attention to the healing power of the springs. He'd find it—somehow.

His bags were sitting by the front door.

Allison was lounging on the sun porch, eyes closed, arms folded tightly across her chest as though she were some pharaoh's daughter laid out in her tomb. Joker shuddered. He did not have a good feeling about this.

"Going someplace?" Joker slid down into a wicker chair, as close to Allison as he dared, yet far enough away not to be a threat.

She didn't open her eyes. "Not me, you."

"Why?"

"I called the nursing home. The business office explained exactly how much Gran's nursing care is costing. They also explained that her income barely covers her care. There isn't anything left over to keep up the estate. You'll have to go."

"Why?"

"I appreciate what you've done here in the house, Joker, but we're probably going to have to find some alternative. I simply can't afford . . . I mean I'll have to delay any repairs to the house until I'm able to skate again. Letting you pay for your board by gardening is one thing, but incurring any expense in refurbishing the estate is out of the question."

Joker considered his arguments. She needed him, but she was proud. She'd never accept his help without a good reason. He knew that the last thing she expected to hear was that legally he already owned the estate. Yet there didn't seem to be any other answer. If he didn't tell her the truth, she'd find out some other way. And what was worse, if he couldn't figure out a way to be close to her, he couldn't help her walk again.

"I really need to go on living in the carriage house," he began carefully. "And you don't have to worry.

You don't have to pay me. Bringing Elysium back to life is a labor of love."

"Why, Joker? Why have you been so good to Gran?"

"I could tell you about a small boy who dreamed about having a real home and a grandmother who told him stories and made chocolate chip cookies, but I don't suppose that would make much sense to you. Let's just say that Mrs. Josey was lonely, and I was lonely. We filled each other's needs."

"I'm sorry, Joker. I know you've been good to Gran, and I don't really object to your living in the carriage house, but the truth is Gran and I need a tenant who can pay rent," Allison said quietly.

She was trembling, holding herself tightly to maintain her fragile control. The sound of loneliness in his words reached out to her. She understood, and she was ashamed that a stranger had been there for her grandmother when she hadn't. But she was there now, and she'd find a way.

"I can't leave," he said softly, making his words a plea as he searched desperately for an answer that would satisfy her. "I have to stay here. There's a debt involved." That much was certainly true.

"What kind of debt? Are you in some kind of trouble?"

He didn't want to tell her. He'd tried to protect her, shield her from more hurt until she was stronger. But she wasn't going to let him do it. Suppose she couldn't take the truth. He sprang to his feet and began to pace back and forth. There was no other way, no other answer.

"The truth, Allison, is that the house isn't yours to rent any more."

Allison went absolutely still for a moment. Her eyes widened as a sudden chill of fear washed over her. What was he saying, not hers to rent? What was happening? "What do you mean?"

"Oh, darling, I'd rather have my arm cut off than have to tell you this."

"Tell me what?" Her voice was a whisper. She curled her fingers into tight little fists, willing herself not to shake. Of course Elysium was hers, or rather it belonged to Gran. Why would he make such a bizarre statement? She shook off the thought that the pain in Joker's face was real.

"Miss Lenice's hospital bills exhausted her funds. Taxes, repair, upkeep on the house had eaten steadily into her savings for the last few years, until there was virtually nothing left. She needed care."

"And?"

"We moved her from the hospital into the nursing home. Once she's recovered a bit more, she'll go into the retirement wing of the center where she'll have her own apartment and there will be someone to check on her. It was what she wanted."

"No."

"The house had to be sold, Allison. Your grandmother's attorney arranged the sale. We signed the papers three months ago, just before she moved into the nursing home."

"No," she repeated, "that can't be true. She would have told me." Allison tightened her lips until they quivered from the strain. She felt as if she'd wiped out in the finals of an important skating competition, crashed with such pain that she couldn't function. She'd never thought much about Elysium, but deep in her mind she'd known it was there. Now it had been swept away. And poor Gran had faced the loss all alone. Allison had been so wrapped up in her own trouble that she hadn't even known.

"Yes, Miss Lenice would have told you. But she didn't want to worry you while you were having a bad time. She wanted to tell you the truth herself, when you were well."

"I see. And the buyer sent you here as caretaker?"

"Not exactly."

"Then exactly what is your position here? Is Gran paying you to be *my* keeper too?"

Joker looked at Allison. Reality had hit him in the heart. The one time he really wanted to make things right, he couldn't. He had only one answer—the truth.

"You're my guest, Allison. Your grandmother sold the house and gardens to me."

Four

"I'm *your* guest?" She looked at him incredulously.

"Please try to understand, Allison. I had to do it. If I hadn't, some developer would have snatched it up."

He was a con artist, a smooth-talking crook. There was no other explanation. Gran wouldn't sell Elysium. Allison wanted to fling herself at the man, scratch the compassion from his concerned gaze.

"He'd have paid more than you, I bet," she said bitterly, knowing all the time that he was telling the truth.

"Possibly, but the estate would have been destroyed," Joker replied, considering whether or not he ought to tell her that the down payment he'd made was part of the creative financing Miss Lenice's lawyer and he had agreed on. It had been precisely figured so that the hospital bill would be paid, leaving monthly payments large enough to supplement Miss Lenice's income later.

"I paid your grandmother a fair price," he said quietly.

"I don't believe you, and I won't let you take advantage of her. I'll sue you!" Allison threatened. She felt a great stab of disappointment. In spite of what she'd been prepared to do to rid herself of the man, she'd honestly trusted him.

Joker inhaled sharply. Eyes blazing with anger, Allison Josey was beautiful, filled with the kind of passion he'd known was hovering beneath the surface. She was hurting—not for herself but for her grandmother. Now if he could just make her turn that passion inward, she'd be well on the road to recovery.

"I can understand what you're feeling," he agreed softly, "but you don't understand. It wasn't even my idea. Simon Cassidy, your grandmother's attorney, came up with the plan."

Allison let his words sink in. Somehow she recognized the truth in Joker's face. He owned Elysium, her home, the very house she was trying to evict him from. "I guess I don't want to understand."

"Ah, Beauty, I'm sorry. I promised your grandmother I wouldn't tell you, but I had no choice. I can't leave. And neither can you."

He'd been standing in the doorway during their tense exchange. Now he walked back out onto the sun porch, dragged a wicker chair closer to Allison, and sat down. She needed comforting, and he wanted to hold her and tell her that everything would be all right. He wanted to, until she gritted her teeth and glared at him furiously.

"So, how did you manage it?"

"I'd rather Simon explain it to you."

"I'd rather you explain it to me."

She wasn't going to make it easy. But then he hadn't expected it to be. He'd hoped he could at least take her hand. Touching her would have cushioned the blow. But it wasn't to be. He sighed and stood up, turning his back as he walked toward the window. Maybe if he gave her the space she needed, she'd listen.

"When I found Miss Lenice collapsed on the kitchen floor, I took her to the hospital. She'd had a stroke. For weeks she couldn't move her right side or speak, but her mind was clear, clear enough to know that she wasn't going to be able to stay here alone."

"I would have come home," Allison interrupted.

"She didn't want to ask you. She thought there was someone you were committed to, and she knew you were dedicated to your career."

"But I should have been told," Allison argued.

"Her doctor tried to contact you, and found out you'd just undergone surgery on your knee. Miss Lenice hadn't known, and they didn't want to tell her how serious it was. You weren't in any position to come then. She thought you'd recover and continue skating, and she wouldn't have it any other way. It was your grandmother's decision."

Allison knew he was right. There was no reason for Gran to believe that she'd ever want to come back home to stay. She'd certainly never given her any indication of how she felt about the place. She hadn't known herself, until recently.

"They told me that she'd fallen, but I didn't know she'd had a stroke."

"You're two stubborn ladies, neither wanting the other to worry. At any rate, the only answer was to move Miss Lenice into the nursing home, where she could recover, and later when she was able to care for herself, move her into an apartment in the retirement section."

"But I still don't understand. Why did she have to sell Elysium in order to do that?"

"You've just been through an operation and a long siege in the hospital. You must know how much things cost. Your grandmother had used up her savings and there wasn't enough coming in to cover her expenses. She's a proud lady. She didn't want to be a burden to you."

"But what about Medicaid?"

"As I understand it, they make all kinds of crazy rules about eligibility. Owning Elysium kept her from qualifying. She's a lady who's always made her own way, so she made the decision to sell. Simon approached me. He knew how much I cared about the estate. If I bought it, it wouldn't be destroyed. Miss Lenice was very grateful, and he drew up the papers."

Allison stared at Joker's stiff back. The reality of his words came crashing over her. All the time she'd been worrying about skating again, about her own crippled body, her grandmother had faced the worst time of her life—alone. What kind of granddaughter had she been?

"I see."

Her sorrow came through in her voice. Joker turned and came back toward her. He cared very much what her opinion of him was. He'd bought the house because there hadn't been any other solution. He'd thought he could find a way to make it right with Allison.

"Ah, Beauty, I'm very sorry. I told you I'd protect you, and all I've done is hurt you. What I did at the

time seemed the right thing for your grandmother."
He gazed at her for a long while, his expression a
reflection of the pain he saw in Allison's eyes. He
reached out and touched her cheek with one finger.

"Don't. I know I should thank you. But I can't—
not yet. I have to go and pack." Allison swept his
hand from her face and struggled to her feet, a tight
grimace twisting her face.

"Where do you think you're going?" Joker reached
down and steadied her, sliding his hand around her
waist.

"I'm moving out of your house immediately."

"No, you're not." He continued to hold her as he
repeated his denial. "That's the last thing you're
going to do. Stop and think about it for a minute. I
promised your grandmother that you wouldn't be
told until she was able to explain it to you. If you
leave here, she'll want to know why, and I don't
think she needs to worry unnecessarily, not now
that she's turned the corner of her illness."

"How will she know I'm gone?"

"This is a small town. It would be all over Pretty
Springs in half an hour. No, you can't go anywhere.
Once you've regained the use of your knee, your
grandmother ought to be well on the road to recovery,
and then we'll tell her the full extent of your injury."

"But I can't stay in the house knowing that it's
yours. Don't you see? I just couldn't."

"You'll have to, Allison."

"No. I'll move into the carriage house, and I'll pay
you rent."

"I will accept from you only what your grandmother
would take from me."

"And what was that?"

"I had to work for my board. Are you game?"

"I don't know what you think I can do to earn my board."

"You can let me help you walk again. You can stay here and let your grandmother see you get well. It'll be all right, Beauty. I know how you're hurting. I'm here, and I care. I really do. You don't have to handle it alone."

Suddenly Allison sagged against him. The tears came, tears she'd held back for so long. She cried for herself, for Gran, for the uncertainty of what was to come. All the while, she absorbed the warmth of the man holding her. The shock of what she'd just learned gradually evaporated, and she felt a faint flutter of hope.

"Why?" she asked breathlessly. "Why are you really doing this?" Her voice was shaking, and Joker knew that she'd crossed over the line that divided fear of what had happened from awareness of him as a man. He just wasn't sure that she knew it, and it took every ounce of willpower he possessed not to tilt her head back and kiss her deeply.

"Because I care about you, Allison Josey. Don't ask me why. Maybe it's because when I came here I'd lost too many people that I cared about, and your grandmother took me in."

"It's easy to care when you aren't the one who's just lost everything."

"No. I lost everything long ago. I guess I'm trying to buy it back."

"I'm sorry, Joker. That was unkind of me. I don't know anything about you or your past."

"Talking about the past isn't easy. Even my brothers don't understand." His voice trailed off. Maybe she'd trust his motives, understand how he felt, if he told her. Maybe he'd understand too.

He caressed her hair with his hand as he talked. "My father was the town drunk. When my sister was only a baby, my mother left us."

"I'm sorry, Joker."

"She didn't live very long. I think she found out that her new life wasn't what she'd thought it would be. After she left, Pop seemed to give up. We'd always lived in housing projects, trailer parks. Toward the end, after my brothers Jack and King were away, we lived in the back of our station wagon."

He paused for a long second before going on. "Finding your grandmother and this house was like finding something I'd lost. And then you came. I care about you, Allison Josey. I felt something the moment we met. Can't we leave it at that for now? I don't know what will happen, or where we'll go from here, but if I could change things and give the estate back to you, I'd do it."

"You would? What if I offered to buy it back at the same price you paid?"

"I'd hate to give it up, but I would."

She knew that he meant it. "Thank you, Joker. I think I might have been wrong about you. I'd like to give you a hug."

She slid her arms around his waist and laid her face against his broad chest. She refused to think about the feeling of energy and power that came with Joker's touch. She just knew that every time he came near her, she experienced an inexplicable yearning. In spite of her hateful accusations, he'd given her a great deal, and she was grateful.

They stood, holding each other, feeling pleasure

in giving comfort. Without thinking, she nudged his shirt away so that she could feel the warmth of his skin against her cheek.

His skin rippled in reaction to her touch. And then the way he held her changed. Her body began to ache with a warm heaviness that she couldn't understand.

"Tomorrow we'll start exercising." Joker cleared his throat and took a deep, steadying breath. Oxygen didn't help. His voice sounded as if it came from somewhere below his kneecaps.

"We will?" She felt dizzy, too disoriented to control the way her body was responding. "Maybe you ought to start by teaching me how to stand. Even my good leg is unsteady."

"I'll hold you." Joker's touch was restrained as he moved his hands reassuringly down her back to cup her buttocks and take all her weight in his hands. He felt her press against him. He couldn't be wrong about the invitation her body was sending him. She wanted him, but now was not the time. If he made love to her now, she'd never forgive him. She was hurt and vulnerable and reacting to his kindness. He'd hold her for a while, let her gently down, and then wait until he knew the feeling was truly for him.

"It's so warm," she said. "We need air-conditioning. I've told Gran for years that we need to get some units, but she would never agree."

"I think we need some fresh air. Let's sit out on the patio and get to know each other." He lifted her into his arms, pushed open the door, and stepped into the cool of the evening. She snuggled close, every brush of her breast against him a form of pure torture.

"Of course, it's your house now," she said agreeably, "and if you want air-conditioning, you don't have to ask me."

"It isn't that simple, darling." He placed her in the swing and sat down beside her, keeping his arm around her. She laid her head naturally on his chest and adjusted her body until they were comfortable together. He didn't think that she'd believe him if he told her that the down payment on the house had taken up all of his savings, that he'd had to make a few good bets at the track to parlay his money into twice what he'd had to start with to have enough.

"Why not? No, don't tell me. I always did ask too many questions."

"Yes, you do. It's so nice and peaceful out here. Let's just sit and enjoy the night."

"All right." Allison leaned contentedly against the man who'd stepped in and changed her life, determined to follow his suggestion. He cared about her. She needed his comfort, and she relaxed as he touched his foot to the floor and moved the swing back and forth.

From where they were sitting, they could watch fireflies twinkle like stars against the velvet darkness of the garden. In the distance the crickets and tree frogs set up a symphony of night sounds, and the ever-present sweetness of honeysuckle and magnolias perfumed the air. A crescent-shaped moon hung low in the sky, sprinkling moonbeams through the branches of the trees.

"How did you hurt your knee, Allison?"

"There's nothing unusual about a skater being injured. You fall, turn an ankle, bump a knee. I'd done it a thousand times—until the Olympics. Then . . ." She went silent for a moment.

"What happened at the Olympics?"

"We were in third place, behind the English and the Russian ice skaters. For some reason we weren't skating well. There was one particularly difficult move we'd practiced, but our coach had decided it was too risky."

"But you did it anyway."

"Yes. We'd completed the move several times back in Colorado. Then in practice I landed off balance and twisted my knee. For the next two days I couldn't even rehearse. They gave me a shot so I could perform and, well, the bottom line is we won."

"But your knee was badly injured, wasn't it?" Joker winced as he considered what she'd said. He'd heard the story before, from every professional sports player he'd met or read about.

"Who knows? In any case, it didn't matter. I had to go on."

"Why?"

"Mar . . . Too many people were counting on me. I would have taken any risk. We didn't have a chance without it."

"And you pulled it off. I saw the pictures of the two of you wearing the gold medals." He didn't tell her that he'd been drawn to that picture first. She had been smiling in the photo, but her eyes had seemed vacant, dulled with the tension of choked-back pain. She'd been hurting even then, and he'd felt her hurt, just by looking at her. The newspapers had said she'd twisted her knee when she stepped down from the box, but he'd known that only sheer willpower had kept her upright during the ceremony and the playing of "The Star-Spangled Banner."

"Yes. We won. We won the gold medal, and it was

worth it." There was a fierce pride in her voice, and the trace of a dare.

"Do you still think it was worth it?"

"Of course," she defended hotly. "How many people in the world have ever been the best—at anything? I may never be again, but for that one moment I was the best."

"Yet even hurt you kept on skating afterward?"

"Yes, we knew that it was only a matter of time before the public would forget about us, and we had to consider the future. It wouldn't have been fair to Mark for me not to go on. We'd worked too hard to quit. After we joined the Ice Follies, we skated all over the world. Even Princess Diana and Prince Charles came to see us."

"And you kept on hurting that knee, didn't you?"

She didn't want to answer him. Even to herself it was hard to justify her actions now. At the time she'd have done anything to hang on to the spotlight and Mark. But now it seemed foolish and terribly sad. Masking the pain had caused her injury to worsen and had cost her the very thing she'd wanted most. Kill the pain? No. She'd never do that again. That's why she'd thrown her medication away.

"What about your partner?" Joker asked quietly after a long moment.

"Mark? Mark and I . . . we split up."

"I know. Where is he now?"

"He's skating with Dance Europe. He couldn't be expected to retire just because I couldn't skate any more. I mean," her voice rose, "skating is his life."

Joker finally understood. Whatever had happened to Allison was more than a knee injury. And if he didn't misread the sudden tension in her body, Mark was still part of her problem. "But why didn't you stop? Didn't you know you were courting disaster?"

"No! Yes. I don't know. Injury is always a risk to an athlete. There's nothing unique about what happened to me."

Joker shook his head. He wanted to draw her back into his arms, but he didn't. Instead he concentrated all his energy on the sadness he sensed in her. As if he were a sponge, he soaked up her fear, and little by little she leaned back until her neck was resting comfortably on his arm again.

"Why did you stay away for so long, Allison? You could have come home any time."

"Joker, I can't answer any more questions. But I'd like to ask you a few. What exactly is it that you do? I can't believe that the income you'd earn as a gardener would allow you to buy this place."

"I'm a gardener all right, but I'm also a landscaper, and"—he pursed his lips wondering how far to go, then decided to tell it all—"and I do a little gambling now and then."

"You gamble? As in playing cards?" She sat up straight and turned to face him. "Why take that kind of dumb chance?"

"It started in order to test my special instincts, and I won. I do it for the challenge, I guess. Why do you skate? For the thrill, the satisfaction of winning."

She considered his answer. "I guess I do understand gambling. The thrill of being the best, of claiming that one moment of glory. I suppose the feeling could be the same. And you won."

"Yes," he added very carefully, "and so did you."

"And now I'm paying the price. I'm not qualified to do anything else, and unless I can skate again, I'll never be able to buy Elysium back. So you see, my answers aren't that simple."

"Nobody ever said life was simple, Beauty." Joker took her hand and held it. "We just do what we have to do. And what we have to do now is get you to bed. Tomorrow we start solving our skating problem."

"This is not 'our' problem, Joker. My knee is my problem, and with the proper therapy, I'm supposed to be able to walk. But skate? Not without pain. And that, I'm learning to live with."

At least she'd voiced the possibility that she was considering some kind of future. He thought she was wrong about the knee. But they'd cross that bridge when they came to it. For now, she was going to stay, and that was all he wanted.

"About that pain. Tell me who issued your prescriptions, and I'll get them refilled. The pharmacist over at the nursing home will handle it for you so that the word won't get out."

"Thank you," she said, knowing that she was going to need the medication if she planned to do any of the exercises she'd been assigned. She gave Joker the doctor's name and told him how he could be located. "I just wish they were magic pills, instead of muscle relaxers and painkillers."

"Oh, you're not going to need them for long. I told you I'd take care of you. Maybe you won't skate again. Big deal. We'll make wings and fly." He gathered her up in what was becoming a familiar position, one hand beneath her legs and the other behind her back.

Hesitantly she slid her arms around his neck. Who was she to argue with her grandmother's judgment? Tonight she needed Joker to be there, too, strong and reassuring.

"Anybody ever tell you that you smell good?" she asked, arranging herself against him.

"Hey, that's my line," he protested, and carried her back inside and up the stairs to her bedroom. "Now I'm going to have to come up with something equally provocative."

"Like what?"

"Like you'd better stop squirming around. It's very stimulating to the male body."

"Ah, Joker, we're friends, remember." As if to torment him, she repositioned her arms and turned her upper body more fully against him.

Joker groaned and dropped his voice into a throaty growl. "You can be friendly in your way, and I'll be friendly in mine. Besides, I remember the first little girl I was friends with. We had a great time playing together."

The upper hall was dark. Joker didn't bother to turn on the switch as he pushed the door open and moved inside Allison's room.

"Oh? What did you play?"

"Doctor and nurse. I always did think that was more fun than cowboys and Indians."

"I'll bet," she said with a laugh. "The cowboy always kissed the horse."

"Definitely a waste of good friendship," Joker's voice had turned husky and was warm against her forehead.

"Aren't you going to put me down?"

"I suppose. Are you sure you don't want to play with me? I'm a lot of fun."

"Not tonight, Joker, my friend. It's beddy-bye time."

"Do I get a good night kiss?"

"Do you think you deserve one?"

"Like your grandmother said, I'm a good boy."

"Good boy? I don't think I'll buy that," Allison said in a light tone. "You're much too charming to be trusted."

Allison never meant to kiss the man. When her arms tightened behind his head, she never intended to lift her lips to meet his. But she did, and when they touched, it seemed very right. She knew that she'd been waiting for him to kiss her all evening. There was nothing urgent about his touch; it was just a gentle examination of her mouth. His mustache feathered her upper lip with a teasing motion. His kiss was wonderful, she thought, as she gave herself over to the sensation.

"Ah, Beauty, I think we'd better stop meeting like this. I mean, a guy could get the wrong idea, standing in a woman's bedroom while she ravishes him with sexy kisses."

"Thank you, Joker," she whispered softly. "For a minute there I almost believed you. You make me feel as if I'm very special. You'd be so easy to take advantage of."

"Take advantage," he pleaded seriously. "I can handle it."

"I'm sorry I was such a witch. I know you're just being nice to me, and to Gran."

"Just being nice? You can tell my body that, lady, but it won't believe you." He dropped a soft kiss on her forehead and deposited her on the bed. "Get undressed, and I'll be back to massage that knee."

"No!" her reply was too quick. The last thing she wanted was for him to touch her again. Every time he held her, she felt as if she were floating. He was definitely addictive. She wanted him to hold her, but she was afraid to let him.

Joker made a rough sound and lowered his head to kiss her again. If she let him kiss her, she'd lose complete control. She had to think about what had happened between them.

"I mean," she blurted out, holding up her hand in rebuff, "I'm so relaxed that my knee isn't even hurting. I think I'll be able to sleep tonight. But thank you, Joker. Good night."

"Good night, Beauty," was his reluctant reply.

"Joker, I wish you'd stop calling me that. I'm no beauty, and you're no beast."

Joker paused in the doorway and turned back to the woman who was showered with silver moonlight as it poured through the window. "Oh, we're Beauty and the Beast all right, darling. But then you know what happened to them, don't you?"

"No, I don't remember. Tell me."

"Beauty turned her back on her past. Then they fell in love and lived happily ever after."

"I think you left out part of the story, didn't you? Falling in love can hurt. Love isn't that simple."

"I guess not. But then nothing important ever is. Beauty and the Beast was a fairy tale about two make-believe characters. You and me? We're real."

"Love is the fairy tale, Joker. And I've quit believing in it."

"I know. I'm going to have to teach you to believe again. Good night, Beauty. Sleep well."

The door closed and she was alone in the moonlight—and she didn't want to be.

By ten o'clock the next morning Joker had gotten Allison's doctor to phone in her prescriptions to the

Pretty Springs Pharmacy, and her exercise schedule was being forwarded to Sandi Arnold, the physical therapist at the nursing home.

Now that the Sports Medicine Rehabilitation Center was fully operational, Joker was beginning to hear the resident athletes' own testimonials about the results of taking the mineral baths. None of the Vandergriffs had believed in the healing power of Pretty Springs when they'd started building the Golf and Tennis Club Retirement Community. The Cherokees had known of the natural mineral springs. According to the information Joker had read in newspapers in the Josey study, people all over the world had believed in the medicinal properties of the springs back in the late 1800's. Doctors in London and New York had prescribed the lithium waters for assorted illnesses with great faith in their success. And the nursing home people swore by them.

He'd get Allison in those waters one way or another. Sandi had said that Allison's therapy schedule was pretty tough. He'd have to get Allison into the proper mood, if he could decide what the proper mood was.

"Be gentle. Calm her psyche," Sandi suggested.

"Appeal to her sporting blood," Kaylyn, whose approach tended to be more aggressive, had argued.

"Just try the old Joker sex appeal," his brother King advised dryly. "It's never failed you yet. But, old buddy, you should decide what you want out of this relationship. Because it sounds as if you might be in over your head."

They were all wrong, Joker mused as he drove. He had to win her complete trust. It was too late to tell him not to fall in love with her. He'd loved her from the time he'd seen her pictures, long before she'd come. He just hadn't known it until he'd lifted her in his arms for the first time. He knew that his feelings were one-sided. She was still getting over the man who'd hurt her so badly. Maybe she was right. Maybe loving was too painful.

He'd loved his mother. He'd loved Ellen. And he loved Mrs. Josey. But that kind of love was different. King's remark stayed with him as he drove his van back to the condo he had been provided with while working on the project, where he stored his belongings. Allison wasn't the kind of woman he usually picked. He liked them strong and successful, sure of themselves. He could be close, love them for a while, and move on before the relationship developed. The women he liked accepted what he had to give and offered themselves in return. The arrangement was always temporary, and they knew it—even Ellen had.

Everyone thought that he'd used the older woman who'd taken him in like a son. Warm and loving, she'd given him direction, and he'd accepted what she'd had to give. In return he'd become her prize student and had given her the son's affection that she'd wanted. She'd expected him to leave her after he graduated, but it had been Ellen who'd gone.

They'd quarreled over his gambling. She didn't believe him when he said that he could put his hands on the horses and feel the energy of the winner, the same way that he could touch a flower and bring it back to life.

She hadn't believed him, and he'd yelled at her. She wasn't his mother, he'd screamed. His mother was dead. He didn't need her to tell him what to do. Then she'd left to teach a seminar at the college. He would have apologized when she returned.

The accident hadn't been her fault. The tractor trailer's load shifted in the curve, killing her instantly when it crushed the roof of her car. But Joker had felt responsible. He'd hurt her and lost her. That's why he'd bought the estate. For once he'd had the right to do something for someone he cared about. And in some way he'd felt that in helping Mrs. Josey, he was helping Ellen, and maybe the mother he'd never known.

Friendship was safer. He'd be Allison's friend for now. They'd learn about friendship together. Then all the rest would follow.

Joker exchanged his van for the red motorcycle he'd left at the center and drove back to Elysium. The house was dark and silent. Allison was already in bed. Joker didn't know why that bothered him, but it did.

He stood in the gazebo in the moonlight listening to the sounds in the gardens. They'd always seemed to accept him and wrap a kind of peaceful insulation around him, but not this night. Allison was inside, and he wanted to be there with her.

He whistled merrily as he walked to the carriage house. But she made no answering call out to him. Only silence echoed through the dark courtyard, and it wasn't a welcoming silence. A long time later he finally slept.

Five

The shrill buzz of a saw cut through Allison's sleep like the screech of a fingernail on a blackboard. She came to her feet, groaned, and fell back on her bed.

"What on earth?"

The noise began again.

Termites. Large, metal, mechanical termites were obviously chewing into the foundation of the house. She caught the brass rail on the foot of her bed and managed to make it to the window. She carefully leaned out and was blasted by the noise again.

"Hey, down there. What's going on?"

There was no answer, only the clatter of falling wood. Allison threw on her robe, reached for her crutches, and began her slow, painful journey downstairs. Somehow she wasn't surprised to find Joker wearing cutoff jeans, laced leather work boots, and a bandanna on his head, wielding a chain saw that was smoothly chewing a hole in the side of the hallway outside the kitchen.

Her heart took a little leap when she saw how the jeans fit his muscular thighs. The seams at the sides were raveling out, exposing a wide expanse of tanned skin feathered with red-brown hair. From the bottom of the stairs she surveyed the earthy man for a long moment as he worked.

"Joker! Jookkeerr . . . !"

It took a couple of screams before she got his attention and he switched off the saw.

"Oh, morning. Guess I woke you up. Sorry, but I need to get this done. They're predicting rain tonight, and I want to get the roof on before then."

"Would it be too much to expect you to explain what you're planning to put a roof on?" She could see behind him into the rose garden through the large square he'd cut out of the wall.

"Not at all. Your new bedroom."

"My new bedroom? I know it's your house, but why are you cutting a hole in the side? Are you planning to move me into the gazebo?"

"Where I'd like to move you is into the carriage house with me. But," he added hastily, "what I'm doing is moving your room to the first floor so that you won't have to go up and down stairs."

"If you'd told me last night, I would have only made one trip down this morning, instead of using the stairs as a revolving door." Allison began to sway. After four days of being back on crutches, she still couldn't keep her balance. How in the world could she control the great hulk if she couldn't even stay on her feet?

"Sorry, it didn't occur to me until this morning. Of course, I'd already planned to build a sun room. I'm just going to expand it. Later, we'll fill the room with plants and wicker furniture. You'll love it. Now you just sit down over here and have some freshly squeezed juice."

"Just for the sake of argument, assuming I approve of your crazy idea, how do you expect to build a room and put a roof on it before it rains? You aren't Superman."

"Of course I don't intend to do it alone. I have help coming."

Allison blanched. "You have workers coming here?"

"Ah, darling, don't worry about it. They won't bother you. I promise."

"It isn't that. It's just that you . . . you can't afford to have a room built on the house right now."

"Don't worry. I have a friend in the building business," Joker assured her, turning her to the breakfast table and seating her in the nearest chair. "You didn't want the world to see you, so I'm building a therapy room here, and we'll use the whirlpool and the baths over at the mineral springs at night. Before you know it, you'll be running up and down these steps the way you used to."

"All right, Joker. If you insist on doing this, I want to help. I'd determined to pay rent. I'm not completely destitute."

Joker recognized the finality in her tone. "All right, Beauty. We'll work out something. You can buy the food. How's that?"

"That's fair. And, Joker, I'm sorry about not believing you. I spent all yesterday doing some hard thinking. I found grandmother's bank statement, and she has exactly one hundred and twelve dollars and thirty-six cents in her account."

"So? That's probably a hundred dollars more than

I have in mine. What does she need money for anyway? Never fear, darling, we have enough money to transform the sun porch into a therapy room."

"I see. And we have money to hire the Sports Medicine Center for my private use only at night?"

"Well, no," Joker admitted, "I'm afraid that I have another confession. We're using the springs free. I'm sort of a friend of the owners. Now drink your juice, and take two of the vitamins in the big bottle. We'll mix a spoonful of wheat germ in with your juice."

"Joker! Don't put me off. Where did 'we' get the money to build a room on this house?"

"These are just vitamins, Beauty. Don't worry, I'd never do anything to hurt you. We're going to build this room on with lots of help from my family and friends." He put his hands on the table on either side of her, and leaned down. "Just relax, Beauty, everything is going to be fine. Joker's going to protect you from the world. Remember?"

"But you're a gardener," she protested, "not a builder, or a social worker, or a . . . whatever it is you think you are."

"I'm whatever you need me to be," he said softly.

It was there again, that same wonderful feeling that came to her every time she was close to him. It didn't invade her senses; rather it quietly swept over them like an invisible heated fog. She felt muscles and nerve endings take on a warm glow. He made her feel as if her body knew a secret, as if it were content to wait until her mind understood the truth.

"But I don't understand. Why are you doing this?"

"Just consider it part of your therapy, less painful

than the treadmill and more satisfying than the whirlpool."

She could see the emotion playing in his face. She pushed his arms away from her and stood. "Listen, you. I agreed to cooperate, but I didn't agree to . . . to . . . who appointed you my doctor anyway?"

She was doing just what she'd sworn not to do, let a man run her life again. Allison fought against the spell he was weaving. She had to get away. She'd go to the nursing home and tell her grandmother that she was leaving. Gran would understand. She always had. Forgetting for a moment that she didn't have her crutches, Allison took a step, felt the explosion of pain in her leg, and crumpled to the floor.

"Ah, Beauty." Joker caught her and crushed her to him, holding her as if he expected her to evaporate into smoke and float off into the air.

She didn't have the strength to fight him. "Joker," she said as she leaned her head against his massive chest and allowed herself to rest. "Joker, I can't fight you. You're too good to me. But I can't let you get more in debt for me. Promise me that you won't do this again."

"I promise that I won't go into debt, Beauty." He wanted to tell her that the supplies and the workers came from his family business, but he held back, fearing that knowing a Vandergriff had bought Elysium might make Allison even more leery of his motives.

"And please call me Allison," she insisted, lifting her head so that she could make certain he wasn't putting her on.

"I'll try, but I may forget. I've called you Beauty for so long that it's become automatic."

The good feeling of being in his arms blurred her thinking, and she knew that she was giving in to him again. Drawing on all her sense of dignity, she tried to pull away—tried and failed.

"Joker, please. You haven't known me for very long. You might not even like me."

"Oh, yes I have," he whispered. His large hands splayed across her lower back, and she felt them tremble. "I've known you forever. Miss Lenice told me everything about you. I even know about the little mole right here."

Joker's hand slid forward, finding the dark spot beneath her right breast as though she weren't wearing clothes. His thumb circled the mole, and she felt the silence of the morning closing out all sense of time and place.

"No," she whispered.

"Yes." He lowered his head. "Good morning, Allison, darling. I like the way you look when you wake up, all mussed and expectant. I think I have to kiss you," he said in a raspy voice, "now."

She swayed against him, as a flower turns toward the sun. And his lips came down on hers. He tasted of coffee, and his beard smelled faintly of sawdust.

He'd cast a spell over the house and gardens. And Allison was caught up in it. Try as she might she couldn't seem to put the breathless feeling of enchantment aside. In all her years of creating a fantasy on ice, that was the magic element that had been missing, and she'd never understood until Joker touched her. She felt as if she were spinning, floating, moving through a beautiful musical interlude, and her feet hadn't left the ground.

Her knees weakened, and she allowed him to

support all her weight. His hands lifted her so that he could deepen the kiss, and she felt his maleness boldly throbbing against her lower body. Her stomach fluttered wildly, and without realizing what she was doing, she slid her arms up and locked them behind his neck.

His lips left her mouth and moved over her face, leaving a trail of heat across her eyelids, her cheeks, before he found her mouth once more. Allison clung to him, feeling the involuntary undulation of her body as his hands matched her rhythm.

She gave in to the delicious feelings of warmth and excitement that racked her body. She felt him move, lifting her until she was sitting on the kitchen countertop, her legs spread to allow him to move between them. His hands found her breasts and covered them.

"Ah, Beauty," he murmured, "it was meant to be like this. Open your eyes and tell me that you want me to love you."

"Love?" Allison forced her gaze away from the gray eyes that were mesmerizing her with gentle persuasion. "No, I can't. You have to stop."

"Stop what?" He moved his lips back again, slower, giving her a quick, thorough kiss.

"Kissing me. I don't come with the house, you know." Allison rolled her head back and looked into a face filled with passion. "You can't want me," she whispered thickly.

"But I do. I've wanted you from the first moment I saw you. I won't hurt you. I promise. We're a team now."

"Yes, you will." She stiffened and pulled herself away from an embrace so perfect, she couldn't tell where she ended and he began. "I can't, Joker. I don't want to go through that again."

Allison felt Joker's hands tighten on her body. She couldn't tell him that for years she and Mark had worked to become a team. From children they'd become fumbling, frustrated teens, learning about their bodies and about desire heightened by forbidden touching and secret kisses. She'd been sixteen the first time Mark had made love to her. The experience had been awkward and painful. She'd accepted Mark's statement that it was her fault. But the experience had bound her to Mark in a way that commitment never had. She'd fallen in love. And because of that feeling of belonging, she'd accepted the lovemaking, though Allison sensed that everything wasn't just what it could be.

Leon, their coach, had tried to separate them, until he saw a way to use their relationship to tune their bodies into a sensual visual expression of their desire. He'd taken Allison for birth control pills and had turned a blind eye to what was happening. They'd been potential Olympic champions, and he'd done whatever was necessary to get them to the top.

Allison couldn't force herself to tell Joker that, but she did want him to understand about Mark. Maybe once and for all he'd accept the truth and put aside his romanticized picture of her.

"I didn't tell you everything before, Joker, about how I hurt my knee. It was at the Olympics that I first realized Mark was unfaithful. His dark, mysterious good looks attracted the other women skaters and fans. And for the first time he was aware of his star power. He wanted to win, and I couldn't refuse Mark anything. The twist, as Leon christened it, was a new move that we thought would set the judges on their ears. If we won, I thought Mark would come back to me."

"But you told me the move was risky?" He knew what her answer would be before she said it.

"Yes, for me. When I fell in rehearsal, we couldn't let the officials know how bad my knee was, or we'd have been cut from the program. Mark slipped out and found a local doctor to give me a steroid shot in my knee."

"That's legal?"

"Cortisone to reduce inflammation is legal, up to a point. Mark said it would be all right. Then Leon arranged for the official doctor to give me another injection. He didn't know about the first one. Both shots deadened the pain, and by the time our event came up, I could skate without feeling anything. We won the gold medal, and Mark did come back to me—for a while. But nothing was ever the same again."

"I see."

Joker's words were guarded. Allison knew that he was waiting for her to continue, but he didn't press her.

"And when we joined the ice show," Allison finally continued, skipping over the four years during which she'd learned to turn a blind eye to Mark's little trysts, "we became officially engaged."

"But you didn't get married."

"No, Mark kept putting it off."

There was such pain in her voice that Joker was sorry he'd asked. Yet he knew that purging herself of such negative memories was part of the healing process, and Allison needed to talk about her ex-partner.

"What happened?"

"I fell again. We had an ugly scene. Mark wanted to bring in another skater to take my place—only until I was well."

"But surely you had an understudy with the show?"

"Yes. But you see, he'd had another offer."

"What kind of offer?"

"With Dance Europe. After our season was over he was going to Europe. He was leaving me at home to recuperate, give my body a chance to heal."

"But you didn't stop skating?"

She had, for a time, until she knew that Mark wasn't going to come back for her as he'd promised. Then, hurt and angry at his deception, she'd taken refuge in the only thing she knew—skating.

"No. After I recovered enough to skate again, I skated alone. Until that last night when even the spectators heard the crunch of my knee when I fell. I left the show and went straight to Boston for the operation. So you see, Joker, everything about me is damaged. I'd only disappoint you."

He frowned and caught her chin in his hand. "You'd never disappoint me, Beauty." He stroked her cheek and bent to place a light kiss on her lips. "Believe me. I know you better than you know yourself. Let me show you."

Allison pulled her face from his grip. She took in a deep breath as she tried to quench the wildfire that seemed to leap through her body.

"You don't understand, Joker. I'm not what you think. You're creating a fictional character, a product of your imagination."

"All right," Joker said with determination. "You're as ugly as a stick, and you're not my type at all. Does that make you happy?"

He was grinning broadly, rubbing her upper arms with his rough hands. How could a simple motion seem so sensual, she wondered. How could a big man with a beard turn her body into mush? She'd always wanted a slim, graceful man with drama in his eyes and the wind in his hair. And Joker? He was a man of the earth—powerful, strong, and stubborn. Allison shook her head. She didn't know anything anymore.

"That may be the first honest statement you've made, you . . . you beastly man! Now, put me down."

"Where I'll put you is at the breakfast table so you can eat!" Joker lifted her from the counter and swung her around. "Ah, Beauty, don't fight me. I only want to help you. Can't you trust me?"

"I wish I could, Joker," she said softly. "But I'm not very confident of anything or anybody right now. Trusting people hurts."

"I wish I had him here in these hands!" Joker's voice went threatening, and Allison felt his fingertips tightened on her shoulders.

Allison jerked her head up in panic. "Who?"

"Mark, the man who sent you skittering off into oblivion convinced that you're an inch lower than a triple-toed mugwump. I'd like to pull his antennae off one millimeter at a time."

"His antennae?" Allison felt her lips twitch.

"Well, that's as good a name as any for what I'd like to amputate. A little pruning is good for the soul." He gave Allison one last brief kiss and turned back to the stove. "I've made coffee and put it in the thermos so that you won't have to get up. There's bread in the toaster right next to the juice. You remember the nice fruit juice filled with natural wheat germ and vitamins."

Allison shook her head in mock defeat, lifted the glass of juice, took one swallow, and gagged. "Yuck! This isn't orange juice, this is yellow mud, thick, gooey, yellow mud."

"Drink it, Beauty. It'll make you grow up to be strong and healthy and," he said with a leer, "I'll let you in on a secret. I have it on the best authority that it's nature's own aphrodisiac. Stimulates hormones and passion, and makes your hair grow."

Allison giggled. "Is that what you've been drinking?"

Joker picked up his saw and did his Texas two-step out the door. "I'll never tell."

A loud noise cut off the end of Joker's comment as a large delivery truck backed into view.

"Aha! Here's Mac and the boys."

"Who's Mac?"

"He's the Pretty Springs Golf and Tennis Retirement Community construction supervisor, and he's a good friend. If you're going to do a job, get the best advice possible," Joker said sincerely.

Allison shook her head in despair as she watched a dark-haired slim young man open the door of the truck and slide to the ground.

"Morning, Joker."

"Yo, Mac. Good to see you."

"Here's what you ordered: two-by-fours, paneling, plywood, and shingles. Two of the boys are right behind me. The princess in her tower?"

Allison watched Joker frown and motion toward the house. The two men spoke in low voices for a moment. They were joined by two other workmen who began unloading the truck and stacking the supplies next to the brick patio. Through the morning Joker worked steadily alongside the other men, pausing now and then to spot Allison through the windows or the hole in the wall.

Mentally she tallied up her savings. She was practically broke. Where on earth would she come up with enough money to pay rent for any length of time? Guiltily she swallowed the vitamins Joker had laid out, as though that might in some way show her good faith. The yellow mud seemed to be a bit more palatable as she drank. Actually, by the time she took the last swallow, she was beginning to develop a liking for the juice.

After watching the walls take shape and the roof become a solid structure, Allison realized that she was beginning to ache unbearably. Reluctantly she swallowed the pills from the prescription Joker had managed to have refilled. She knew she ought to drive into Pretty Springs to visit Gran, but she couldn't get her car past the big truck.

After a telephone call where she learned that her grandmother was making another trip to bathe in the mineral springs, Allison left a message that she'd be by for a visit in the morning.

Allison's plan to move to a lounge chair where she could watch the work in progress more comfortably was aborted when she stood and felt a wave of dizziness overtake her. She sank back to her chair and contemplated a long nap instead.

Joker watched Allison's head begin to droop. She was getting sleepy. Good. Her body needed rest, lots of rest. He nodded to his helper, moved lightly into the breakfast room, and lifted Allison once more. She sighed and curled her head against him as he walked.

Upstairs Joker laid her down, lingering for a moment to push a strand of soft dark hair away from a face innocent and lovely in sleep. Planting a light kiss on her forehead, he backed away and returned to his construction.

After a quick sandwich and icy sweet lemonade for lunch, Joker and Mac went back to work. It was late afternoon when the final piece of roofing went into place and the rain began to fall. By the time Joker had cleaned up and returned to the kitchen, the rain was coming down in torrents, and Allison was standing in front of the open door staring out into the garden.

"What are you doing, Beauty?"

"Watching the rain fall. I love to watch the rain and the snow. Everything is clean and pretty afterward. When I was in the hospital, I used to wish I could run out and let the water make me pretty."

"You want rain, Beauty, you got it." Joker swooped her up and walked through the open hole in the wall and into the garden, swinging her round and round in a circle. The rain pelted them, soaking their clothes and hair in seconds. It made little rivers down his face into his beard and turned Allison's long lashes into spikes that dripped crystal beads of water.

"You idiot," Allison said, laughing. "We're getting soaking wet. I feel the way I did when I was a child and Gran turned on the water sprinkler for me to play in. Except I didn't play in my clothes." She held her face up to the water as if she were a parched flower.

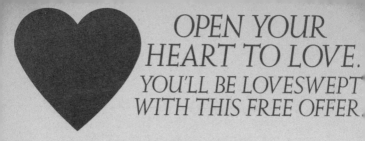

OPEN YOUR HEART TO LOVE. YOU'LL BE LOVESWEPT WITH THIS FREE OFFER.

HERE'S WHAT YOU GET:

1. FREE! SIX NEW LOVESWEPT NOVELS! You get 6 beautiful stories filled with passion, romance, laughter, and tears... exciting romances to stir the excitement of falling in love... again and again.

2. FREE! A BEAUTIFUL MAKEUP CASE WITH A MIRROR THAT LIGHTS UP! What could be more useful than a makeup case with a mirror that lights up*? Once you open the tortoise-shell finish case, you have a choice of brushes... for your lips, your eyes, and your blushing cheeks.

*(batteries not included)

3. SAVE! MONEY-SAVING HOME DELIVERY! Join the Loveswept at-home reader service and we'll send you 6 new novels each month. You always get 15 days to preview them before you decide. Each book is yours for only $2.09 — a savings of 41¢ per book.

4. BEAT THE CROWDS! You'll always receive your Loveswept books before they are available in bookstores. You'll be the first to thrill to these exciting new stories.

BE LOVESWEPT TODAY — JUST COMPLETE, DETACH AND MAIL YOUR FREE-OFFER CARD.

FREE – LIGHTED MAKEUP CASE!
FREE – 6 LOVESWEPT NOVELS!

- NO OBLIGATION
- NO PURCHASE NECESSARY

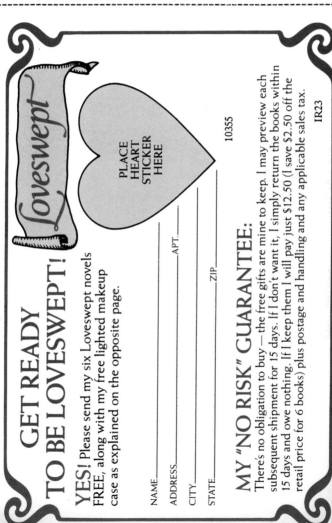

GET READY TO BE LOVESWEPT!

YES! Please send my six Loveswept novels FREE, along with my free lighted makeup case as explained on the opposite page.

PLACE HEART STICKER HERE

NAME_____

ADDRESS_____APT._____

CITY_____

STATE_____ZIP_____

10355

IR23

MY "NO RISK" GUARANTEE:

There's no obligation to buy — the free gifts are mine to keep. I may preview each subsequent shipment for 15 days. If I don't want it, I simply return the books within 15 days and owe nothing. If I keep them I will pay just $12.50 (I save $2.50 off the retail price for 6 books) plus postage and handling and any applicable sales tax.

(DETACH AND MAIL CARD TODAY.)

REMEMBER!

- The free books and gift are mine to keep!
- There is no obligation!
- I may preview each shipment for 15 days!
- I can cancel anytime!

(DETACH AND MAIL CARD TODAY.)

BUSINESS REPLY MAIL
FIRST-CLASS MAIL   PERMIT NO. 2456   HICKSVILLE, N.Y.

POSTAGE WILL BE PAID BY ADDRESSEE

Loveswept

Bantam Books
P.O. Box 985
Hicksville, NY 11802-9827

NO POSTAGE
NECESSARY
IF MAILED
IN THE
UNITED STATES

"Well." He stopped and grinned at her. "We can take care of that in a heartbeat. Wanna get nekked?"

"Too late. We're not children anymore."

"Speak for yourself, Beauty. I never intend to grow up. Playing is good for the soul. Look how beautiful we've become. Look at us, Allison. Don't you see?"

She gazed at the burly man with the strong arms. "Yes, I think I do. You never see the ugly in life, do you?"

"Never. If I don't like what I see, I just find a different way of looking at it."

"I wish I had eyes like yours," she said seriously, "Eyes that see beauty in everything."

"You want new eyes? I'll make them new, if you'll let me."

She hugged him, pushing her face into the shelter beneath his chin. "Maybe you can, you crazy man. Maybe you really can."

An early morning call from the Chattahoochee construction site took Joker Vandergriff reluctantly away from the estate. He didn't feel good about leaving before Allison was awake. The previous night had seemed to be a milestone in their relationship. He'd taught her to accept him, and he'd wanted to stay close to her.

He looked in on her before he left, taking in the relaxed way her hand lay against her cheek. Satisfied that she'd sleep very late, Joker called and delayed Mac and the construction crew's arrival until lunchtime before heading to the office to settle the delivery date for the junipers he'd ordered and to check the planting schedule for the sod.

Later he stopped by the glass company to be certain that the glass panes he'd bought would be delivered and installed in the new sun room. The last stop was the nursing home, where he found Miss Lenice bright-eyed and eager to share the news of a second visit from her granddaughter.

"Take care . . . Joker," Lenice had managed to say, and he'd known she wasn't warning him. She understood that something was wrong with her granddaughter, and she was passing on that problem to him just as she had her home. He'd nodded and had spent the next twenty minutes keeping up a nonstop patter of nonsense about frying chicken and planting marigolds. When Mrs. Josey began to tire, he pressed a kiss against her forehead and left. She hadn't had to ask him to look after Allison. He'd accepted her as his responsibility the moment she'd fallen into his arms in the gazebo. She needed his help just as much as the gardens he was slowly bringing back to life.

After leaving the nursing home, Allison drove past the old grammar school she'd attended. She had fond memories of that time in her life, when Gran had walked her off to school and kissed her good-bye at the door.

When she'd awakened earlier, she'd felt better than she had in a year. For the longest time she'd waited for the sound of Joker's footsteps. But the house had been silent. Finally she'd realized that she was alone—totally alone—and she'd missed her red giant. She'd lounged around all morning waiting for Joker to return.

Days before she'd demanded that he leave, and he'd ignored her request. Then he'd gone, and the house had become a tomb, until the phone had rung, and the angry voice had demanded to know where Joker was hiding out. She'd imagined terrible things. Suppose he didn't come back? She really would be alone.

As the hours dragged by she became restless. Finally, she'd folded herself back into the small red car she'd spent her first paycheck on and driven to the nursing home. She'd even managed to get into Gran's room and settle into a chair before Gran woke from her nap. Gran was glad to see her, but she hadn't fooled Allison for long. After several glances around the room, Allison had answered her unasked question.

"Joker isn't here, Gran. He had some business to take care of today. Did he tell you that he was building a room on the house off the dining area?"

"Yes . . . sun room will be . . . nice."

"You approve?" Allison tried to keep the sound of dismay from her voice.

"Yes. Joker knows best."

She wanted to ask her grandmother why she sold the house, but she took one look at her and knew she couldn't. Asking about money was totally out of the question. She settled instead for questioning her on Joker's rebuilding plans.

"Gran, you like Joker, don't you?"

"Yes . . . good person. You?"

"Yes," Allison admitted, "but, do you think it's a good idea to let Joker spend his money on me? I mean, well, he didn't even discuss it with me. He just cut a gaping hole in the wall and went to work. Is he always so stubborn?"

Lenice Josey's eyes lit up. She nodded her head and managed a half smile. "Always . . . if he loves you."

"Loves me? Don't be silly. He's a man who loves dirt and rain and moonlight. He probably loves worms and insects too. If he doesn't, well, he'll just blink his eyes and they won't be there."

"Yes. Joker's . . . special man."

When one of the staff members came to change Gran's bed, Allison managed to slip out the door without calling attention to her crutches. She planned to call back later and make an appointment to discuss Gran's condition with her doctor. She couldn't leave everything up to a stranger, even if the stranger was a special man.

And Joker was a special man. Ever since she'd stepped into that gazebo, her world had changed. She'd come there seeking solitude and had run into a man intent on invading every part of her life. He was so different from Mark. Mark was temperamental and demanding, the man she'd spent the last years of her life trying to please—and he'd never smiled the way Joker did. They never had taken time to play in the rain or cook hamburgers on a grill. Every part of their life had been spent on working toward perfection of an illusion.

Only now did she understand the truth. Illusion came from inside. It couldn't be manufactured or orchestrated. It was a reflection of the soul's most intimate desire. Joker had known that instinctively. Joker, who saw only beauty, was showing her the eyes of her soul.

Allison had to do something in return.

The Bolton Boys Ford dealership came into view as she drove. It occupied the corner where the ice rink used to be. Allison pulled in. They paid her cash for her car and arranged to have someone drive her home. She hadn't stopped to think why she was doing it. She'd just sold the car, collected the money, and gone home to wait for Joker.

One company problem led to another, and it was late afternoon before Joker exchanged his motorcycle for his van and returned to the estate. He knew Mac Webster and his workers would be gone, but he hadn't expected to find Allison's MG missing from the driveway. Allison couldn't be gone. She wouldn't have left without telling him. Joker felt a slash of pain invade his chest as he raced inside.

"Allison . . ."

Six

"... Allison! Allison!"

There was no answer. Joker's pain seeped into every one of his pores and turned into an icy fear as he tore up the stairs into Allison's room and jerked open the closet door.

"Thank God! She left her clothes."

"I doubt they'll fit, but whatever turns you on, big guy." The amused voice came from behind him.

Allison, wrapped in an oversize bath towel, was standing in the bathroom doorway supporting herself on one crutch. Her hair was still damp, though it was obvious that she'd been drying it. She'd been in the shower and hadn't heard him call. She hadn't left. Joker breathed a long sigh of relief. "Your car is gone. I thought ..."

"Yes." She made her way over to the bed and sat down clumsily. "Where have you been all day, Joker? I was ... worried."

She was worried about him. His heart rate took

off again. He could smell the fragrance of the soap she'd bathed in. Through the terry cloth towel he could see the clear outline of her nipples. Even as he walked across the room and stood beside her, he didn't understand the great need he felt to hold her. "Why?"

"A man called here looking for you. He said that you were doing some work for him and that you were late. He sounded angry and said if you didn't get over there, he'd send Chief Newton for you."

King, no doubt. His brother had just vented his displeasure that Joker wasn't there and hung up. Solemnly Joker lifted her and sat down on the bed, placing her knee across his thighs with the intention of examining it. Just touching her set off warning bells in his head, and he tensed his muscles. *Take it easy. She doesn't know how you feel.*

"I didn't know what to tell him."

"Who?"

"The man who called. I was afraid that you've been spending time helping me when you should have been somewhere else."

There was a catch in her voice. She'd tried to protect him. Joker felt a great wave of tenderness wash over him, and he shifted her so that she was in his arms. She curled against him and hid her face in the curve of his shoulder. Her body seemed to belong there.

She felt fragile, as though he were holding some delicate shell. Her heart was thudding against his chest, and he knew that he was in trouble again. The sweet scent of her invaded his senses, and he squeezed his eyes shut as forbidden images captured his imagination.

"Hey, don't worry, Beauty," he said, making swirls across her shoulder with one hand and grasping her knee with the other. "He wasn't serious. It was just my brother, being cute. I had some family business to oversee, which I did. Nobody is going to bother us here." *Don't touch her*, he told himself. *Don't start something you can't finish. She's in need of simple comforting. Forget that she's nearly nude and burrowing herself against you as though you were her last refuge.*

"What about Chief Newton?" Allison asked softly as she felt his hand slide up her leg and rest on her thigh. Awareness of what she was feeling sifted through to her. She was tingling all over with a curious warmth that seemed to have no central source. Everywhere her body touched Joker's, she felt her skin vibrating. Now he moved his hand back to her knee, and the tingling sensation accelerated. She felt as if her leg had been asleep and was coming back to life.

"Of course, I could be in trouble with Chief Newton. He doesn't hold with compromising a lady. For that he usually starts with messing up a person's face," Joker ad-libbed flippantly. "Then if that doesn't work, he goes on to other things, like chopping off fingers and toes, nothing too drastic, you understand, just little subtle suggestions to get your attention."

Hell, what was he saying? He didn't know. She'd turned his mind into mush, and he'd lost any sense of reason as he breathed in the sweet fragrance of her hair and touched the satiny skin that came to life beneath his fingertips.

"Don't worry. Joker can always take care of himself,

and you, too, my Beauty." His hand slid up her arm and came to rest on her breast.

She gasped. What was she doing draping herself all over this man, allowing him access to her body? No, that was wrong. She was inviting him to touch her. She took a deep breath and tried to push herself away. "I'm not worried," she insisted.

"Ah shucks, and I thought you'd been sitting here all day missing me. I thought that's why you might be glad to see me."

"Well, I'm not. I don't care if you go out and get your fool head cut off." She wrapped her arms around his neck, lifted her head for a moment, and smiled. "I was just worried about your fingers."

"My fingers? You're worried about my fingers?" His voice sounded unnaturally high. He wouldn't want to do without his fingers either. Without his fingers he couldn't touch the body he was holding. He couldn't run his fingertips down her backbone or caress her upper arm or hold the small round breast beneath his hand. He couldn't tangle his fingers in her damp silken hair and turn her face up to his. He couldn't . . . Lord, what was he doing? The woman was turning him into a fumbling kid. He'd never wanted anything as much as he wanted to rip the towel from around her and press her back on the bed beneath him.

"Why shouldn't I worry, you big dear man? Do you think you have a monopoly on worrying about people?"

"Nobody worries about Joker."

She caught his face in her hands and held it so that she could look into his eyes, eyes that were veiled, moist, not piercing as they'd been that morning in the garden, but slightly confused as if he were having trouble believing her. And she knew in that moment that he was as vulnerable as she. He was tough, yes. But he needed reassurance just as much as she did. And now she could give something to him.

"I do. How much money do we need, landlord?"

"Money? Eh . . . too much. Why?"

"Because you're adding on a room when you should be repairing the house. I can't allow that, Joker. Letting me stay here is one thing, but what you're doing is too much. I figured"—she paused and took a deep breath—"that I couldn't drive anyway, so I sold my car."

She released his face and reached behind her. Joker heard the rustle of paper and felt her touch as she pulled his arm from around her, slid her fingertips along its brawny girth, and placed a stack of money into his palm.

"You sold your car? Why?"

"Don't worry about that, just use the money. I can't move in and let you support me without contributing to the expenses. I insist on sharing the costs. You take the money. It's for you."

"You sold your car to pay me rent?" Disbelief shattered what little control Joker had left. "You sold your car for me?"

"What are you, a broken record? Yes. I sold my car. I didn't think it was going to be of much use to me. And anyway, that's what . . . friends are for, isn't it? You did say we were friends, didn't you?"

"Ah, Beauty . . ." He couldn't speak. He only wanted to hold her. "Why'd you go and do a thing like that?"

"You've been good to Gran, been here for her when

I wasn't. I wanted to let you know how I felt, and I didn't know how."

"A simple thank-you would have been enough. You didn't have to do this." How could he tell her what a beautiful unselfish gesture she'd made?

"I've never been able to express myself very well, unless I'm on the ice, and that isn't likely to happen again, so? Ah, hell, Joker, don't make this any tougher than it already is. Take the damned money and get out of here before I do something dumb like cry."

She'd touched some secret part of him, and he hadn't expected that. He was the giver not the receiver.

A tenderness filled his chest and spilled over into his mind so that all he could feel was an incredible need to touch her—but that's what he'd been doing, stroking her leg and hip while his lips placed light little kisses down the side of her face and behind her ear.

"Oh, Beauty, you're an extraordinary woman. How good it will be to make you well so that I can show you exactly how wonderful you are, but I can't accept this money. It would be dishonest." He laid the stack of bills on the table and put his arms back around her. "I have to tell you—"

"Please, Joker," she interrupted. "I have to give something to you, and you're going to have to accept it." She tightened her arms around his neck and turned her face back to look at him. In two days he'd invaded her life and her thoughts to the point that she couldn't think of anything else.

And suddenly, all the bad memories went away. Her eyes fluttered open as he lowered his head, and without any thought of refusal, her lips parted. Slowly, almost delicately his lips touched hers. She gave herself over to the taste of him, felt his restraint, and loved him for it. He nibbled around her mouth, sighed, and lifted his head.

"I've missed you," he said huskily.

"Ummm. Do you give all your boarders such special treatment?" She tightened her arms around his neck and laid her face against his chin. His beard and mustache caressed her skin deliciously, and she was drawn deeper and deeper under his spell.

"Only those with great dark eyes and pixie faces," he said, teasing, giving himself over to the joy of holding her.

Once he'd kissed her again, she was scarcely aware of what she was doing. Her heart beat wildly, and she was filled with joy. "You're right," she whispered dizzily, "you've turned this into a magic place." The buttons on his shirt were suddenly open and the thatch of red-brown hair seemed irresistible. She moved her cheek against it and was rewarded when he involuntarily shuddered.

"Yes," he murmured, incredibly shaken as he tried valiantly to subdue the longing she inspired. "And the magic will make you walk again, without that crutch. All you have to do is believe."

Walking was the last thing on her mind at the moment. The towel had come untied, exposing her breasts to his intimate touch. He brushed his hand over her nipples, rosy with desire. She flung back her head and moaned.

The sound cut through the silence, jerking Joker out of his dreamy state. He shook his head and pulled back, separating himself from her with a sigh of regret.

"Dammit, Allison, this is not good."

"It isn't?"

He set her away from him, mumbled a curse, and pulled her full length against him one last time, letting her feel the heat of his desire openly before he drew back. "Allison, I'm sorry. I mean . . . I can't seem to stop touching you. I know that's what I promised, but I don't know if I can sit here just holding you much longer."

"You can't? Why? I like it. I like it very much." She made a move to reclaim her place in his arms.

"Ummm," he said with a groan. "I'd like to be six years old and playing doctor again. But I'm not, my Beauty. And right now this poor old frustrated body knows firsthand that you aren't wearing anything under this towel, and it's cursing my promise to be just your friend with a vengeance."

"What's wrong with friendship between two bodies?" Allison asked, feeling the wonderful sense of peace she'd come to expect when Joker touched her.

"At the moment our friendship is very one-sided. My body is more into lust. Stop squirming around."

"I can't seem to be still."

"The flesh is weak, darling, at least most of mine is. You'd better let me work on your knee, before I forget what I'm here for and ravish you."

He moved her from his lap and put his hands gently on her knee without any pretense at massage. Suddenly the stiffness in her leg disappeared.

Allison gave a moan of contentment and moved back into his arms, encountering a part of Joker's body that didn't appear to be weak in the least.

"Oh! Joker, when I'm with you my body seems to reach out and meld itself to yours, and I feel as if I could do anything as long as I'm touching you. I never thought I was a very . . . sexual person. Do you want to make love to me?"

Did he want to make love to her? She was lying in his arms wearing nothing but a towel, and she asked if he wanted her. "Oh, yes, Allison Josey. I want to make love to you."

"Then why don't you?"

"Don't do this, Beauty. This isn't a good idea, my love. It was just that your beautiful gesture, selling your car, made me a little crazy. Now this . . ."

Joker was burning with sensations. Allison's fingertips were skimming his chest with quick little motions as if she were memorizing every inch of him.

"Joker," she whispered hesitantly, "if touching me all over is good for my circulation, I don't mind. I really think that the stimulation is working. Could you touch me again?" She took one of his hands and moved it slowly back up her body to her breast. The catch in her breath broke the silence and Joker's last shred of restraint.

He felt as if he were tumbling out of control. "Don't do that, Beauty," he said gruffly, and slid her feet to the floor as he sprang from the bed and walked to the window, calling on every overworked ounce of willpower he possessed to instill some semblance of rationality into his shattered body.

"I'm sorry, Joker," she murmured. "I didn't think. I mean, you just make me feel so good."

A voice from within roared at him, silencing his mind and regathering his control. "That's good,

Beauty. I want you to feel good. That's part of healing." And one of these days, he was going to show her how wrong she was about a lot of things, beginning with walking and ending with sex.

"Do you have a swimsuit?" he asked, his voice making him sound like a cross between Kermit the Frog and Foghorn Leghorn.

Allison's voice was having its own difficulty as her body went from burning hot to frosty. "No. Well, maybe. I have a maillot, a bodysuit that I suppose could be considered a bathing suit. Why?"

"We're going to take a little trip to the springs. Where is the suit?" Joker moved toward the chest of drawers.

"In the bottom drawer, but Joker, you don't really believe all that stuff about those mineral springs, do you?"

"You'd get into big trouble if Minnie and Luther Peavey heard you make a statement like that. Pure blasphemy, woman."

"Who are Minnie and Luther?"

"They're the most shining examples of the springs' healing power. They were both invalids in the nursing home before they ran into Kaylyn and discovered her springs. Now they're the most vitally alive eighty-year-old married couple I know. You ought to remember Miss Minnie. She used to be your neighbor."

Allison searched her mind. "Miss Minnie Rakestraw, next door?" She vaguely recalled a large rawboned woman who popped in and out of Gran's kitchen without any warning. "I think so."

"Well, she and Luther got married several months back. They were causing a regular scandal in the nursing home until the director agreed to let them get married and share a room legally." Joker held up a dark blue metallic French-cut bodysuit and grinned. "This it?"

"Yes, but I don't want to meet anybody, and I have no intention of wearing that thing to take a swim."

"Suit yourself darling," Joker said with a shrug of his shoulders. "If you'd rather swim without, I'm game." He lifted Allison, maillot, towel, and all and started down the stairs.

"Put me down, Joker. I am not going off on a motorcycle wearing nothing but a towel."

"Well, you could leave that behind, but I think Chief Newton and the Pretty Springs police department might object. Besides, we're not riding my bike tonight. We're traveling by van."

Joker pushed open the door and revealed the sleek bronze-colored van parked in the driveway.

Allison gasped. "Joker, how did you afford such a van?"

"Well," he hedged, "it's not paid for, if that's what you mean."

By the time Allison got over the shock of the luxury vehicle she'd been ensconced inside, Joker was driving smoothly onto the highway. She glanced around, noting the bed in the back, the ornate lighting fixtures, and the bar. "This isn't a van, Joker, this is a bordello. How many women have you ravished back there?"

"I'll never tell. But I hope we don't have an accident," Joker said wryly. "We'd make a catchy item for the front page of the Pretty Springs *Gazette*."

"At least this time I've got my man," Allison quipped before she realized what she'd said.

Joker took a quizzical look at Allison. He wondered

what the basis was for her odd remark. There was a suggestion of pain on her lips, lips that curled into a little half smile. The oversize towel she'd wrapped around her looked for all the world like an Indian sari. With her bare feet and her dark hair curling around her face, she looked like some exotic mysterious beauty.

"All you need are some jewels and an elephant to become a royal princess. Command me, memsahib, and I'll be your servant for life."

"Oh, Joker. I don't want you to be my servant. I don't want you to build a room on your house or to take me for a swim in the mineral springs. Just be my friend—and," she added impishly, "my personal doctor. It's too bad my doctors at Boston General don't know about your brand of treatment. They'd have patients lining the halls."

Her words brought a surge of instant heat to his groin as he realized what she'd said. He almost missed the back entrance to the springs. It took a sharp jolt of the brakes to slow the van as he turned into the private underground parking area of the Sports Medicine Rehabilitation Center. The center was empty as he'd arranged. He let out a deep sigh of relief and looked over at Allison.

She was staring at him with big dark eyes, eyes filled with trust and something deeper that he wouldn't let himself examine. He wanted her. He'd never wanted a woman more. And he'd never turned away from a woman he knew he could have—until now.

"We're here, Beauty. Let's go inside." He ignored the confusion he saw in her face. She'd allowed herself to respond naturally, and he'd pulled back from her the second time in less than an hour.

"Inside where?" She retucked her towel and drew her old curtain of wariness around her.

"The springs. I'll show you." Joker moved swiftly around the van, opened the door, and carried her into the elevator, pushing the button for the ground floor.

"Are you sure it's all right for us to be here?" Allison whispered.

"Positive. I told you that I was related to the owners. And this is where I work. I was the landscaper for the whole project. I promise you, we have permission to be here. Relax."

The elevator door opened, and they stepped out into a dimly lighted room. The place seemed empty, but she couldn't relax. In the distance she could hear the musical sound of falling water. Joker walked through the rock-walled lobby and over a bridge that stretched across a stream of swiftly moving water.

"Is this the mineral spring?"

"Yep. It bubbles up through these rocks and collects in a pool. The pool overflows and the building is constructed around the path the water takes before it disappears back into the earth."

The sound of rushing water was louder now, and the air seemed tinged with an odd, sulfurous smell. Joker moved into a second room and touched a switch on the wall.

"Oh! It's beautiful." Around the edge of the rocks were soft blue lights that turned the bubbling water into prisms. Hundreds of flecks of light glinted off the rocks like stars in a velvet night sky.

"Now, you can put on that suit, or I'll just slip you right into the pool as you are."

"I'll put on the suit," she answered quickly. "If you'll put me down somewhere so that I can manage."

"Fine. You change in here, and I'll go find a suit for me."

Joker stepped inside an alcove and placed Allison on a stone bench. "Stay put. I'll be back in a minute."

Quickly Allison managed to pull the skimpy maillot on. Uncomfortable with the amount of flesh exposed, she draped the towel around her shoulders and waited, filled with apprehension. How had she allowed him to bring her here? She knew that her protector was raising her hopes for another failure.

When she looked up, Joker was standing in the doorway in a swimsuit that left absolutely nothing to the imagination. His beautiful smile was larger than the scrap of fabric.

"Ready?"

Allison nodded. Her tongue seemed to be stuck to the roof of her mouth, and she couldn't speak. Her eyes were drawn to the thatch of hair that curled wildly across his chest and disappeared below his navel into the suit. She wasn't prepared for so much of him to be exposed. He wasn't a burly giant as she'd thought. He was big, yes, but with a graceful beauty that made her think of a great tawny cat, a gray-eyed, curious cat that swayed back and forth in calm anticipation, ready to pounce on its unsuspecting prey.

She struggled to stand, leaning on her good leg, determined not to let him sweep her up in those great arms.

"You're beautiful, Allison," he said in a husky voice.

His gaze left no doubt in her mind that he was seeing the woman he wanted her to be not the real person she was. But it was the real Allison who felt every hair on his chest touch her with magical tingles of heat as he lifted her and walked into the water until only her shoulders were still above the surface.

"What now?" Her voice was thready and uneven. She sounded as if she were a prepubescent boy whose voice was changing.

"We simply sit in the water for now. Later, I'll massage your knee, and we'll do some exercises."

"Oh, so now we're finally going to play doctor?" Her eyes sparkled with amusement as she allowed the churning water to move her up and down against his body.

"Who's playing?" he said with a growl. The wench. She was actually flirting. He knew that she wasn't aware of how close he'd been to losing control earlier. Now, she was taunting him with her body. Hell, he had already lost it. No way he could stop himself if he continued to hold her. He dropped his arms from beneath her legs and let her slide down. The mineral water would hold her up.

"Oh, hell!" He hadn't counted on her sliding straight down his body, clasping his waist, and holding on.

"What's wrong?" She flung her head back and looked up at him, swallowing heavily. "Do you have a cramp?"

He groaned. "Yes, in my libido, darling."

"Shall I massage it for you?"

"I don't think that's a very good idea. I don't think this is a good idea either, but I can't seem to stop myself."

He lowered his mouth to hers, unable to stop himself.

"Oh, Joker," she tried to say, threading her hands weakly through his hair. He was holding her, kissing her, and the water lifted her up against him, her legs shifting so that one slid between his.

"Oh, Lawdy, Miss Claudie," he drawled between kisses, "we're doing it again. This is heaven."

"Yes, we are," she responded, curling her legs around his, "and we aren't at home either."

The gentle undulations of her body against him did wicked things to his control, and he stopped kissing her and lifted her upward so that her legs were around his waist. He looked down at her with a puzzled expression on his face. "Not at home? What does that mean?"

"You do know that the Josey estate is called Elysium. I was beginning to think that I'd died, and you were a figment of heaven's imagination."

"Elysium, yes. I know. What does that mean?" One hand tangled in her hair while the other hand freed her breasts from the suit.

It wasn't the heat of the water that was scorching her body. It was the man holding her. She felt his lips on her breast, and she gasped, arching her head back to allow him full access to her body. "It's where the Greek gods went when they died," she murmured, "a magical place of pleasure."

"I like that," Joker said as he released one breast and caught the other nipple between his fingers. "There is something magic about the house and gardens."

"It's those crocodiles," Allison announced. "They'll do it every time." She felt her body quiver as his fingers left her breast and moved with whisper-light motions down her body. In seconds her suit was gone, and he was touching her intimately, finding the throbbing center of her desire.

"No, and it isn't magic either, Beauty, it's you and me."

"Oh, Joker, what are you doing?" An unfamiliar heat ignited between her legs, and she let out a cry of anguish.

"Hush, darling, just let the magic work."

The musical sound of the water vibrated off the rock walls, rising and dying down in no particular rhythm. Joker's fingers moved delicately, probing and teasing. Lost in the myriad of sensation she opened herself to him, taking his tongue inside her mouth and his fingers inside her body. Her muscles contracted, and she pressed herself against him.

"Oh, Joker . . . I want . . . I need . . ."

"I know," he whispered, as he lifted her to a rock that bordered the side of the pool and moved his mouth down her body, planting maddening little kisses across her rib cage and lower . . .

"Joker . . ." She clutched his shoulders and opened her mouth, arching herself shamelessly against him. She wanted to scream. She wanted to feel him inside her. She hadn't known she could be so hot. And then she felt it, the roaring tempo of blood rushing to the core of her being. She couldn't stop herself. It was happening, a shattering pleasure that ripped through her and took her breath away. There was only feeling and heat and a breathtaking pleasure that lingered even after Joker had pulled away, lifted her into his arms, and wrapped her in her towel once more.

"That's never happened before," she whispered.

"I'm glad," he answered, and tightened his grip.

"It isn't the house, is it? It's you. Why? Why me?"

"I don't make profound statements very often, Allison, but I'm going to try to tell you something I've never said to anybody. I'm a touching person because . . . because as long as I can reach out and touch someone, I know I'm not alone. People are abandoned in different ways, and they find their own kinds of reassurance. I want you, Allison, and you need what I can give."

Allison stared at the bearded man holding her. He seemed larger than life, and his deep gray eyes reflected an uncertainty that struck a chord in her. "You're not alone, dear Joker. I don't know what I can give in return, but I'll hold off your demons, if you'll hold off mine."

"You've got a deal, Beauty." He grinned, helped her into her suit, lifted her, and walked back to the elevator, leaving a trail of footprints across the lobby floor.

Seven

From the moment they left the center Allison knew that they were going to make love. Her body was both curiously relaxed and zinging with electric impulses. The springs, she told herself, it was the chemical content of the water that made her feel as if she were fire and ice. But she knew that it wasn't the minerals in the water. It was the man beside her.

In the van Joker reached across and took her hand, holding it for a long moment before he released it and started the engine. He didn't speak, and yet she felt the magic of his thoughts reach out and reassure her. Allison sighed and leaned back against the plush velvet seat, closing her eyes and drinking in the ambiance of the night.

Joker saw the soft smile playing over her lips. Lord, she was beautiful. Her wet hair was washed back from her face, calling attention to deep blue-black eyes hidden by thick lashes. Everything about

Allison was regal and mysterious in the streaked light and shadow of the van as they drove down the tree-lined street.

"Are you warm enough?" Joker knew he was driving too fast. "I should have gotten another towel for your hair."

"I'm all right, I think, but you may have a permanent imprint of my . . . me on your seat." Her teeth chattered slightly, and she knew it wasn't because she was cold.

"Happy van," Joker said huskily. "Now you've left your imprint on both of us." He wanted to take her hand and show her how much of an imprint she'd made on him. He'd thought the hardness would go away once he'd stopped touching her, but it hadn't.

He was driving the van down the highway, almost stark naked, aching with need. It was all he could do to keep from stopping the van, throwing her down on the plush bed in the back, and fulfilling the fantasy she'd introduced earlier with her question. Instead, he waited for the first red light, reached out, and pulled her over for a quick intimate kiss that only made everything worse.

"I wish you'd stop kissing me, Joker. You make me want . . . No, that's a lie. I want you to kiss me. I like you to touch me. I like the way you make me feel. I just wish I didn't."

"There's nothing wrong with what we feel, Allison. It isn't often that two people find each other as we have. Why does it bother you so much?"

"It's hard to explain. I feel as if you're a figment of my imagination. I don't even know your real name."

"My name is important to you?"

"No, not exactly. But the name Joker is wrong

somehow. I know it. I think there must be some reason why you'd rather I call you Joker than tell me the truth."

Joker felt a sinking sensation in his stomach. The truth? Hell's doorknobs, for too long he'd just said whatever made things easier for the person he was dealing with. He wasn't sure that he could be completely honest. Or could he? How would she feel if she learned that he was one of the Vandergriffs? Maybe if he started at the beginning.

"Why not? Okay, I'll give it a go. With no supervision I was a pretty wild kid. I'm lucky I didn't end up in some juvenile home."

"I guess I am too," Allison whispered under her breath. "You mentioned your father drank."

"That's saying it nicely. I told you that my mother left us. Then Pop died when I was sixteen. Or that's when his body quit. He gave up a long time before that."

"It's bad, not having a mother. I was lucky. At least I had Gran."

"Maybe. I don't know. My sister Diamond doesn't remember mother at all. Neither do I, really. Except every now and then I'll catch a certain smell or touch something soft, and for just a second I can see her. And then she's gone."

"Having to raise four children must have been hard on your father. How did he manage the baby?"

"He didn't. He had a sister that kept her while the rest of us were in school. Afterward, one of us took care of her. Most of the time it was me. I was five years older. You'd be surprised what an enterprising fellow can do with a baby as a front."

"Joker!"

"Well, there are lots of kindhearted people in the world willing to help a motherless infant."

"Did your brothers know what you were doing with that innocent child?"

"My brothers handled not having a mother better than I did, I guess. They went to school and to work, anything to keep from having to come home. Then, when Diamond was eight, Pop's sister took her permanently."

"What about you?" The more Allison heard about Joker's childhood the more she understood how important Elysium and her grandmother must be to him.

"Me? Oh, she offered to take me, too, but I couldn't leave. Somebody had to take care of Pop while Jack and King worked."

"I wish I'd known you then. I think we could have been friends."

"Oh, I don't know. You probably wouldn't have liked me. I was a first-class jerk. To cover up my insecurity I became a clown, a hustler."

"So that's where you got the name Joker. But what did your mother call you?"

"My mother gave us respectable names, but there was a time once, when Pop had a sense of humor. My oldest brother Arthur became King. The next in line, Jackson, became Jack. My sister's real name is Lillian. Pop changed that to Diamond Lil and finally to Diamond."

"Jack, King, Diamond, and Joker. Your father must have been a gambler?"

"Yes. Not a very good one, I'm afraid."

"And the queen?"

"That was Mother. My dad called my mother

Queenie, until the day he died. We were supposed to be his royal flush. Except he never made any money, and we weren't even good luck."

"But the names stuck."

"As I got older and Pop got . . . sicker, I took my name seriously. I really hustled for money. Joker just seemed to fit my life-style."

No mother or father? She could understand that. All she knew about her father was that he'd been a marine. She'd pretended that he was a wonderful, handsome young man who'd been killed in some senseless training accident without ever knowing that his sweetheart was pregnant. But that was all pretense. The only thing she knew for certain was that an automobile accident had taken her mother less than a year after she'd been born. If it hadn't been for Gran, she could have suffered the same fate as Joker, perhaps worse.

"You told me your brothers' and sister's names, but you didn't tell me yours. Tell me now. What is your real name?"

"James Daniel Vandergriff," he finally said in a rush, "but nobody has ever called me anything but Joker."

"Vandergriff, as in the firm that built the Golf and Tennis Retirement Community and the Sports Medicine Rehabilitation Center?"

"Yes. Are you upset that I didn't tell you in the beginning? I was afraid that you'd be angry about my buying the estate, since my family is in the development business."

She moved closer and laid her hand on his bare thigh. "Angry? No, I'm not angry. I know you love Elysium. Thank you, Jamie."

All sad thoughts went right out of Joker's mind. "Jamie?" He almost choked. "Really now, do I look like a Jamie?"

"You look exactly like a Jamie, a big, sweet, lovable, Jamie."

"Well, I like the lovable part anyway." If the hand circling his thigh took any wider a path, she'd find out just how lovable he was prepared to be.

"Tell me about the real Jamie. What makes him special. I need to understand."

"I'd rather discuss the sweet, lovable part of me," he said with a grin and leaned toward her.

"I'd rather hear about the wicked part of you. Tell me why you need to gamble when your family owns the springs. You don't really need money, do you?" She gave his thigh a squeeze of encouragement.

"No!" His voice was too loud. But in giving her squeeze of approval, her hand was playing a wild game with the rest of his body. "I'm not really a gambler. I don't just gamble. I mean I do, but only when it's necessary. I mean, it's never for me. I've only gambled for somebody else."

"Like me? Would you gamble for me, Jamie?"

"Well, yes, but . . ." He pulled his attention from the fingertips drawing little electric circles on his bare leg, and tried to give her the answer she deserved. "I don't know if you're going to believe this. I don't talk about it, but I seem to have some kind of sixth sense that gives me feedback. I mean, when I touch something, I can feel a positive or a negative response. When I get that positive feeling, I just know that it's right."

"For instance when you touch my knee. You can feel some kind of . . . energy there that responds?"

Joker looked at her in shock. "Yes. That's it exactly. How'd you know?"

"I feel it too. It's as if you create a kind of heat field that acts on the weakness. But what does that have to do with gambling?"

Joker left the main road and turned into the driveway of the estate as he considered his answer. He was going to have to put something into words that he wasn't certain he understood. Even his brothers and sister didn't know the truth. He stopped the van in the courtyard near the back door and killed the engine.

"I'm not sure, Beauty. But when I go to a horse race, the animals seem to respond to me. If I can get into the stable to touch them, I just know which one will win. The same way I can touch a flower or a plant and I'll know which one needs me. If I touch it often enough, it will respond and grow."

"And that's why you keep touching me?"

"That's why I touched you in the beginning. Now? I touch you because I need to." He took her shoulder and turned her to face him, slipped the other hand under her chin, and tilted her face upward. "Don't you feel how much I need you, Beauty?"

"Yes," she admitted breathlessly, moving her hand from his leg to his chest. "I think I'm beginning to understand. It's just that I've never been a touching person. I'm nearly twenty-seven years old and except for Mark, I've never been with a man."

"I'm glad."

She lowered her head and smiled. "I don't know how to tell you, Jamie, but it's different with you. I go crazy when you touch me, even though Mark said I was cold. Sometimes you're overwhelming."

"I am? I don't mean to be."

"Yes, you do, and," she whispered unsteadily, "and I think I'm beginning to understand why."

"You are?" He drew in a deep breath and brushed his lips across hers.

Her hands moved slowly down his chest to his hips. He was driving her crazy, and he knew it. She wanted him to feel the same conflicting emotions she was feeling. It was time to drive him a little crazy.

Allison grinned, took a deep breath, and spoke her words in a rush before she lost the courage. "The problem is the swimsuit, Jamie Daniel. I really think you ought to take it off."

Joker couldn't breathe, and he was sure that his heart had completely stopped.

"Take—it—off?" He hadn't heard her right. She couldn't be inviting him to strip naked in the front seat of his van.

"Either that," her voice cracked foolishly as it trailed away, "or get one two sizes larger. I think this one is definitely cutting off the flow of blood to your head."

The ripple of his chest beneath her touch strengthened her purpose. "Dreadful for the circulation. And it isn't good for the thinking process either." She trailed her fingertips downward, across his navel, across the part of the suit that was definitely being stressed to the maximum, and back to the chest. "Let's go inside, Jamie."

Joker felt Allison shift to the other side of the van and heard the door open. She'd touched him. She'd deliberately reached out and put her hands on his pulsating body. The woman was slipping over the edge. It had to be the lithium water in the springs—some kind of reverse kinetic effect. Hell, she'd practically invited him to . . . what? He didn't know. His brain wasn't functioning because all his blood was in one throbbing part of him. All he knew was that he was sitting in the van like some dumbstruck kid.

"Ah, Beauty. I think you're probably right about the swim trunks. What exactly did you have in mind?"

"Well . . . I'm not sure. Those springs of yours are certainly invigorating. I'm hungry. I think I'd like some fried chicken. What about you?"

"Fried chicken!" Joker's voice exploded, "You're hungry? For food?" The problem with the swimsuit immediately vanished as he opened the van door, strode to the other side, and opened it.

Allison swallowed hard. Saying it out loud was suddenly difficult. She wanted to feel him against her, inside her.

"You really do want to make love to me, Jamie, don't you? You're not just doing it as part of my therapy, are you?"

"No! I mean yes, I want to make love to you, and no, it isn't part of any therapy." His voice was almost harsh in reply. "But I won't touch you unless you're sure. Be sure, Allison. Before I take you up those stairs, be sure."

Allison knew that he was offering her the opportunity to say no. He wouldn't force her, though they both knew full well that all he had to do was kiss her, and she'd give in without a protest.

"Kiss me, Allison. Let me know that you want me too." The quiet desire in his voice played on her senses at the same time the heat of his body permeated every pore of her bare skin.

Allison felt a giant shudder in her body as though her heart and her lungs took a second to gear up in anticipation of what was to come. She answered him the only way she could. She kissed him.

He didn't tighten his grip as he felt the rush of fire hit him somewhere in his lower stomach. He forced himself to stand totally still in the darkness, allowing only his lips to speak. The melting rush of feeling changed as she tentatively slid her tongue into his mouth. Her boldness excited him, and his breath quickened as her arms slid up to encircle his neck.

Allison pressed herself closer, tangling her hands in his hair, across his mustache, through his beard, moving herself against him in a spiraling urgency that mirrored the rhythm of her tongue. She felt her heart beat wildly. She wanted to feel the downy hair of his chest next to her body. She wanted to touch him, all of him. She moaned, pulled herself away from his lips, stripped the swimsuit from her body, and pressed her nipples against him.

This time the moan came from Joker as he returned her kiss for an urgent moment. He was on fire, burning up in the heat of his desire for this woman. Standing in the darkened courtyard, he knew that he'd passed the point of no return. He had to have her, and he knew that no matter what she thought about herself, she wanted him too.

Lifting her to him, he whirled around and walked up the steps to the carriage house. Inside the bedroom he carried her to the bed and let her slide down until her feet touched the floor.

"Can you stand for a minute, darling?"

She caught the post at the foot of the bed and steadied herself. "Yes."

As he pulled his arms from around her, she gave a light gasp and listened as he walked across the dark room and pulled open the drapes, letting the moonlight flood the floor and the bed behind her.

"No," she whispered dazedly as she licked her swollen lips.

"No?"

"I mean the drapes. Leave them closed."

"Not this time, my Beauty," he answered. "I want to see you, and I want you to see me."

"You might be disappointed with me," she said hesitantly.

"Not a chance, darling, just look at yourself. Your nipples, they're all swollen, throbbing, waiting for me to caress them with my tongue." He knelt before her and began to stroke her legs and thighs. She could feel his warm breath against her body. When he took her nipple inside his mouth, she moaned and held on to his shoulders.

He gently fondled her breasts, licking, stroking, turning her nipples into hard little buds that burned with fiery heat, until she rocked against him shamelessly.

"Slowly, Beauty. We'll touch and taste and learn to know each other." He rose, and she felt suspended in mid air, her heart hammering in her throat. He caught her waist and looked down at her. She couldn't see his face, but she could feel his gaze on her. And the urgent frenzy disappeared as she waited, replaced by *the* feeling—that warm, special feeling that came over her whenever he was close. She took a deep breath and let it out.

"Yes." When she gave a hesitant smile, he slid his hands up until his thumbs touched her breasts and his long fingers were splayed across her back.

"Just relax, my love. I'm going to kiss you. You like the way I kiss you, don't you?"

His hands were flexing against her body, like a pianist limbering up his fingers to perform. Each suggestive ripple sent off a message along the network of nerve endings beneath her skin. With nothing more than his hands, he was changing the composition of her body, and she felt herself take a step closer.

"Jamie?"

"Yes, darling. Let yourself feel my aura. Our bodies are synchronizing themselves. Can't you feel the pull?"

He was right. She needed to feel his bare skin against hers again. His hands began to move, and their imprint set off a tingle down her legs to her toes.

"Wait," she murmured, inserting her thumbs beneath his trunks and working them down his body. His arousal throbbed insistently between them, and she pressed herself to him. Everywhere she touched seemed warm and vibrant.

Joker pulled himself slightly back and moved his chest back and forth across her breasts, brushing her nipples with his chest hair until she wanted to cry out with pleasure.

Joker cupped her bottom in his big hands and lifted her from the floor, sliding her up his body until he was able to reach her breasts with his lips. She felt his velvet-soft mouth close around one taut nipple, and she couldn't hold back her cry. The great beard and mustache caressed and tantalized. His lips greedily pulled as if he wanted to take all of her inside his mouth.

Joker continued to lift her up and down, cradling his erection between her thighs with his movements. Her lower body grew moist and hot, and suddenly her legs were clasped around his hips and she arched toward him with a deep moan.

Allison was on fire. She wanted this man. She was throbbing, groaning. She knew now what had been missing in her life. Her breath came in short quick little pants as she felt some great coil of heated desire began to twist inside her. Desperately she ducked her head and forced his lips to meet her own. She felt as if she'd never kissed a man before. Kissing Joker was a promise of what he could do to her body. With his tongue he examined her with a maddening slowness, sliding it in and out of her mouth as he demonstrated what was to come. Just as she reached the end of her endurance, he removed his tongue and made her give him hers.

The coil of heat inside her lower body was drawn tight, and she felt herself begin to lose control. Tightly she contracted her muscles. She couldn't let go. She didn't know what would happen, she had to hold back. The pain, the need . . . And she heard the moan of anguish. It was Joker. And then she knew that whatever she was feeling, he was feeling too. This great, burly man was holding on to the last thread of restraint. He wanted her as much as she wanted him.

"I can't wait much longer, Beauty," he said, breathing as though he were behind some glass wall, suspended in a soundless vacuum. "Is it all right?"

"Oh, yes. It's wonderful," she said, panting. "I never ever knew it could be so wonderful."

He laid her back on the bed, catching the edge with his knees and supporting his weight with his elbows. He slid inside her, pausing for her small frame to adjust to his size. He entered her until they fit together as naturally as if they'd been designed as two parts of a whole.

"Yes, yes, love me, Jamie."

"But I haven't protected you," he said, trying to slow the involuntary motions of his traitorous body.

She gasped. "Please?" Tightening her legs around his thighs, Allison lifted her body to follow his attempt at removal. "Don't. Please . . . please don't stop."

And then it was too late. The explosion that enveloped them was a fiery eruption of sensation that tore them apart and flung them back together again into a shimmering orbit of pleasure. Wave after wave vibrated outward until the fire melted away into a steady core of warmth.

Only when the flames began to die down and she came back to her senses did Allison realize that she was holding on to Joker's hair with both hands and her legs were locked around his great thighs. Only then did she feel the throbbing of her knee and the weight of the man still holding her breast with his hand and still joined magnificently to her lower body. She couldn't hold back a slight moan as a spasm tightened her knee.

"Damn!" Joker rolled away. "I forgot about your leg. I seem to have forgotten about everything."

As he pulled himself away, she felt a great wave of regret. "No," she whispered, and knew the whisper was more of a plea. "Don't leave me."

"Ah, darling, I'm not leaving you." He slid up on the bed and drew her into the curve of his arm. Threading his fingers through the silk of her hair, he spread it across her shoulders until he found her breast and clasped it possessively.

"Rest your leg across me, and I'll warm it."

Obediently she turned on her side and moved her leg across his thigh. As she did she felt moisture trickle down between them. "Oh!"

"Don't be embarrassed, darling. I'm responsible for that. It's us, you and me, our bodies letting us know how good we are together. Don't ever be embarrassed over making love with me." He shifted her upper body until she was practically lying across him.

"Yes," she whispered, caressing him lovingly. There was a joy in being close, a wonderful rightness about loving him. She smiled in the darkness and placed a kiss on his chest. She didn't know how to express her feelings about what had happened, about the miracle, the pleasure that she'd never dreamed she'd experience. But with Joker she didn't have to. He knew how awkward she'd felt, and he understood the wonder of her surprise. This was making love. This was what she'd been cheated out of. She sighed in satisfaction.

"Did I hurt you?" Joker asked, cursing himself for his impatience, for forgetting about her injury in his great need to love her.

"Oh, no." She ran her fingers across his chest, skimming over the wiry hair. She wasn't shy anymore. The intimacy they shared had changed all that. "My whole body feels so wonderfully relaxed that if you weren't holding me, I'd float away."

"Are you sure?" He moved his hand down her rib cage to her knee. She didn't flinch at his touch, and he couldn't feel any tension as he tenderly probed the swollen joint.

"Honestly. I'm not sure why, but my knee feels . . . it feels," she searched for a way to describe the detached feeling, "as if it's floating in water—warm, bubbling water, like in the springs."

"Me and the springs. Seems we both have healing power. What do you know about that?" Joker's hand rested lightly across her kneecap, and he felt an answering throb of response.

Allison didn't know how to tell him, but she knew that the heated vibrations beginning again stemmed not from bathing in the springs but from being close to the man holding her. "The springs may be powerful," she began hesitantly, "but I don't think they hold a candle to what's happened here. It's you, Jamie Daniel, your loving touch."

"Whoa now, Beauty, you're just feeling the after-glow."

"Afterglow?"

"When the loving between two people is very good, there is an afterglow. If we're lucky, it will stay with us for a while. If we're very lucky"—He kissed her eyelids—"it will stay with us . . ." he started to say forever, but amended it to, "all night." From her ear he skipped down her neck and across her collarbone, hovering just above her left breast until she thought she'd die of anticipation. Then he captured her nipple and tugged it into his mouth.

"No. It's you," she said, giving herself over to the delicious sensations bursting to life again. "I'm not very good at loving. It has to be you and the magic."

Joker released her nipple. "Beauty, loving you was so wonderful that you made me forget everything. I don't think I could have stopped, even if you hadn't been protected."

"Protected?" She mouthed as his lips nibbled at the corners of her mouth.

"Yes, protected." He kissed her again as his hand left her knee and found the most tender part of her. "As in birth control, darling. Don't be shy with me now. This concerns both of us. What are you using?"

"Oh, that?" She sighed as he turned her onto her back and lifted himself on his elbow over her. "I don't use anything."

"What?" Joker sprang to his feet like a wounded bear. "Allison, tell me you're joking."

"You needn't worry, Jamie." Her voice turned sad as she explained, "I can't have children."

Joker didn't know whether he was relieved or angry. He'd just made love to a woman without making certain she was protected. Yet she was saying that she was sterile? She was wrong. He didn't know how he knew, but he did.

"What makes you think that, Allison?"

Allison took a deep breath and made up her mind to answer him. "I can't talk with you standing there glowering at me, Jamie. You make me feel . . . awkward, ashamed."

Joker heard the uncertainty in her voice. No matter how disturbed he was at what he'd done, he couldn't make her uncomfortable about their having made love. He lowered himself to the bed and stretched out beside her, settling her back against him. He took a deep breath and allowed the feel of her to work at erasing the tension her words had caused.

"There was a time," she said hesitantly, "when I wanted a child, Jamie. I thought a child would make everything right between Mark and me. But sometimes women athletes have trouble conceiving. After they've exercised and worked at their sport for a long time their bodies stop functioning correctly as women. I'm a woman who couldn't have a baby, and I'm a skater who can't skate anymore. I'm a complete, all-round failure."

"You want to have a child?"

"No, not any more."

"You mean that you don't want me to give you a baby?" Joker's voice went soft, and his body began to die a slow death. "What do you want, Allison Josey?"

"What do I want? More than anything else I want to show the world, myself, that I can skate again."

She'd said the world, but he knew that it was Mark she wanted to show. She still cared about the man who'd caused her injury and deserted her. He could understand that. They'd shared so much for so long.

Mark was the one hurt he hadn't been able to erase. He could feel the tension in her body. She was holding him as if she were afraid that he'd disappear, and he didn't think she was aware of her grip. He nuzzled her cheek, pulling her face up so that his beard was a cushion for her chin.

"Skating. Is it that important to you?"

"Oh, Joker. He was supposed to come back. He promised, and he never even called me again. It's taken me a while, but I understand him now. Oh, yes. I want more than anything to skate again."

"I see."

Suddenly she felt Joker's stillness. What had she said? She hadn't meant to let Mark's meanness touch Joker. For so long she'd refused to think about Mark and what had happened. She'd kept the past bottled up inside her because it had hurt so much. But this night she'd torn down all the walls. Joker had given her the confidence to let herself face Mark's treachery, and she'd voiced her humiliation over his rejection.

Had she spoken aloud? She seemed to remember angry words. Oh, Lord, she hadn't even been talking to Joker. How could she explain what she was just now beginning to see?

Joker felt his heart rip into little pieces. After what they'd both shared the thing she wanted most was to skate again. To skate again so that she could run back to the man who'd hurt her so badly. The closeness, the joy, they'd just experienced meant nothing. Well, if that was what she wanted, that was what she'd get. He'd make certain that she skated again. Where he'd played at healing before, this time he'd prove it, to himself and to Allison.

Sadly she looked up at him, waiting for whatever he was going to say. "I'm sorry, Jamie," she said in a voice barely above a whisper. "I didn't mean . . ."

"That's all right, Beauty. You want to skate again,

and I'll help you. I'll get your training room ready. Starting tomorrow morning, be prepared for a schedule that will make you think that training for the Olympics was child's play."

"You don't understand," she began. "Let me explain." But the coldness in his eyes stopped her. "Please don't do this, Jamie."

"Jamie isn't doing it. Jamie is a gentle, foolish man who loves you. He couldn't help himself. You were right about him, but you were wrong about me. I told you, my name is Joker, and I'm about to show you, Allison Josey, that when it's necessary, a Joker can be very wild."

Eight

"Hello!"

Wham!

"Yoo-hoo! Allison."

Wham! Fram! The whole house shook from the pounding.

Allison groaned, stretched, and forced open her eyes. What in the world was attacking her front door? Even Joker's mechanical ants made less noise.

"Get up, Allison. We're late. Open this door."

Allison looked over at the clock beside her bed. Eight-thirty. Oh, no. She felt as if she'd just closed her eyes. For the three days since Joker had made love to her in the carriage house, she'd worked at her therapy during the day until she could barely move, soaked in the mineral springs every night, and slept badly if at all.

"Go away! Whoever you are, I don't want any!" Allison sank back to the bed and covered her head with her pillow.

Wham! Wham!

Whoever it was didn't intend to go away. Allison sat up. It didn't make any sense. Why didn't Joker open the door? He'd paraded the world through the estate since her crash therapy had begun. Where was the stern red giant now that she needed a houseboy? Allison swung her feet to the floor and reached for her robe. Her crutches were resting at the foot of her bed. She pushed her hair out of her eyes and got up.

"Just a minute! I'm coming," she called out, leaving one of her crutches behind as she made her way to the foyer. It was probably another trainer or someone from an equipment company delivering more steel for the torture chamber that Joker had erected in the sun room. If it was another muscle-bound hulk, there to give her a lesson in stretching techniques, she'd have him string Joker up to one of those shiny chrome exercise bars by his toes.

Allison paused. Other than the banging on the door, the house was quiet, the vacant, empty kind of quiet that she could identify with. She'd heard enough silence in the last six months. She was alone. Maybe Joker had taken her seriously. Maybe he'd given up.

"Allison, Joker will have my hide if we don't get to work. Please! Open the door."

It was Sandi, the therapist from the nursing home, she realized. Allison pulled her robe on, unlocked the door, and opened it a crack.

"I'm sorry, Sandi. I must have overslept. Come in. Are you alone?" Allison looked around. She didn't know whether she was glad or sorry that Sandi was alone. Every time she looked up, Joker was standing in the background, frowning, pushing, urging her on. He drove her crazy when he was there and even crazier when he wasn't.

"Joker said to let you sleep in for a while this morning. But Minnie sent fresh blueberries and pancake batter for your breakfast, so today I'm the cook."

"Thanks, Sandi, but I'm really not hungry."

"Doesn't matter. Minnie said to cook, and I'm going to cook. Joker will be along soon. I saw him down by the road, climbing that old dead tree. I told him he was going to break his neck, but when has Joker ever listened to anybody? I guess you know that better than anybody, don't you?"

Though Sandi was probably the same age as Allison, she looked like a teenager. Her blond hair had been caught up in a jaunty ponytail, and she was wearing a pair of white shorts with a yellow T-shirt. Sandi was the perennial cheerleader—enthusiastic but tough. Allison suspected her nonstop conversation was designed to both reassure and distract patients.

Dropping her bag on the counter, Sandi turned back, closed the door, and practically propelled Allison into the kitchen. "Sit down, Allison, and I'll pour you a cup of this hot coffee. Pancakes will be ready in a jiffy."

"But Sandi, I imagine that Joker has already had breakfast," Allison protested. "And I really don't feel like a heavy meal."

"I can believe that. Anybody could look at you and tell you haven't been eating enough to keep a crow alive. But that will change now. With Joker's health food menu, you'll do fine. I have to admit that I'm glad it's you who has to eat it and not me."

Allison opened her mouth and closed it again. Talking to Sandi was like talking to a whirlwind. She just swooped round and round until she overpowered you, and you eventually gave up and followed directions. Between Sandi and Joker, Allison didn't stand a chance.

"What was Joker doing climbing a tree?" Allison asked, trying not to let her interest show.

"That's what I asked him. He said something about working out his frustrations by chopping wood. But I never saw anybody cut wood while the tree was still standing."

"He does have his own way of doing things, doesn't he? Did you know him, before my grandmother fell, I mean?"

"Not really. Joker's a bit of a lone wolf. Of course, I knew who he was. I work with Kaylyn. She's Joker's sister-in-law, King's wife. Now there's a couple who're crazy about each other. Of course Joker and your grandmother are pretty close too. After Mrs. Josey moved into the nursing home, Joker was there every day. Why didn't you let somebody know you were coming?"

"I didn't know it myself." Allison forced herself to take a sip of the coffee Sandi had poured. There were so many questions she wanted to ask, questions she hadn't been able to ask before because there'd always been somebody else around. "How long has Joker been here?"

Sandi placed the flat iron grill on the large burner of the stove and turned it on to heat before stirring her batter. "About a year, I'd guess. He came along shortly after Kaylyn mobilized the town in protest over the destruction of Pretty Springs. Of course, nobody expected Kaylyn and King to fall in love and get married, but they did. And they figured out how to save our mineral springs too."

"Somebody else said something about that. Kaylyn really chained her husband to a rock?"

"Yep. He was going to plug up the springs and tear up Lizard Rock. Kaylyn wouldn't stand for that, so we protested. Oh, it was glorious, all those folks picketing to save the springs and Lizard Rock."

"Well, the lizard is still there. I saw it when I drove into town. How did they solve the problem?" The springs were as much a part of Allison's past as the town. But she'd never known they were good for healing. It seemed that Joker knew more about her town than she did.

"They built the sports medicine center in with the golf and tennis community thinking that it would draw big-name athletes in to undergo rehabilitation along with the people who wanted to play golf and tennis. So far, though, the pickings have been pretty slim. The folks over at the nursing home could tell those ball players a thing or two if they'd listen."

Allison cringed. She guessed she was one of those people who had refused to listen.

Sandi added the blueberries to the batter and stirred them gently. "Goodness, I forgot the sugar." She sprinkled a spoonful into the mixture and nodded her approval.

"But what about Joker?" Allison prompted.

"It was Joker who figured out the solution."

"He is pretty special, isn't he, Sandi?"

"He has a way about him, Joker does," Sandi said. "Never saw anything like his flowers. Personally, I think he pirates some of that spring water to douse 'em in."

"The man definitely has a way about him," Allison admitted, remembering the night she'd spent in his bed. She averted her face quickly as she felt a flush sweep over it.

After Joker had stormed out of the carriage house and deposited her back in her bedroom that night, he'd barely touched her unless there was someone else in the room. She didn't know what had happened. After their wonderful lovemaking, she'd said things about Mark that she hadn't known were going to come out of her mouth. And she hadn't known how to take them back.

"Pretty Springs couldn't have gotten along without Joker," Sandi rattled on. "So far as I can tell, he doesn't have a girlfriend. He—"

"He smelled those blueberries all the way down the road." Joker limped into the room.

Allison screamed.

Sandi dropped her mixing spoon and gasped. "Gracious, Joker, what happened to you?"

Joker sniffed, wiped his nose on the shoulder of his shirt, and blanched at the smear of bright red blood. As soon as he'd seen Sandi drive past in the nursing home van, he'd started down the tree he'd been preparing to cut down. Hurrying, he'd put too much weight on one section and the branch had cracked, hurling him through the lower limbs to the ground.

"Your face is cut, and your nose is bleeding," Allison said, her own face going white with concern. "Who hit you?"

"Who? Ah, nobody. I fell. Don't worry, Beauty. I'm not hurt."

But Allison didn't hear his explanation. All she

could see was the purple bruise already appearing on Joker's cheekbone and the dried blood on his forehead. "We need to get an ice pack on that face," she said briskly, forcing herself to her feet. "You come over here and sit down."

"I'll get ice," Sandi offered, turning off the stove and reaching for a fresh dish towel.

Joker looked at the expression of concern on Allison's face and followed her directions. Could she really be worried about him? He'd work it out if he could just get over the peculiar, shifting sensation. He had to reassure Allison. She didn't need to worry about him. Then everything began to fade away.

"Ah, no! Hell's doorknobs." He couldn't pass out, he couldn't pass out, he told himself. He was going to pass out.

"Sandi, Joker's fainted."

"Must have fallen out of that tree," Sandi observed matter of factly. "Well, I'm not surprised. Can't tell him anything." She pulled an ice tray from the refrigerator and emptied it into the towel.

"Oh, Sandi. Look at his face." Allison slid to the floor and let her crutch fall with a clatter. She lifted Joker's head into her lap and began to feel for his pulse. "I'm afraid that he's hurt badly. Look how pale he is. Did you know that his real name is James Daniel?" Allison wiped the blood from Joker's face with her napkin.

She could tell from the expression on Sandi's face that she wasn't making any sense. She didn't know herself what she was saying. She only knew that Joker was hurt, and she was scared out of her mind.

Joker hovered halfway between consciousness and oblivion as he heard Allison's disjointed conversation.

He moaned and risked a peek. Allison handed Sandi the soiled napkin and asked for a clean one. He could see Sandi's face over Allison's shoulder. He shook his head in warning, pleased to see her answering nod.

"Promise me that you won't let him know how worried I am, Sandi," Allison repeated. "He's such a tough guy. I'm sure he will be embarrassed about having fainted. Do you think we ought to call an ambulance to take him to the hospital? He might have a concussion."

"Oh, I don't think that's a good idea. I doubt that Joker would like the world to know that he had a fight with a tree and lost. He's supposed to have a way with growing things."

"He's the most wonderful man I've ever met, and he thinks that I'm an ungrateful shrew. I don't know what to do about it." Allison planted a soft kiss on his forehead and anxiously patted the wet cloth to a cut on his forehead. "We have to get him to the hospital, Sandi."

"Maybe we ought to get the doctor here," Sandi suggested. "Joker . . ."

". . . isn't going to see any doctor," he said with a groan. "Beauty, it's no problem." Joker flexed his neck and snuggled closer. "I think all I need is to be still for a minute. Everything is whirling around. Please, just hold me."

"It's all right, darling," she whispered lovingly, "I'll take care of you."

Darling? She'd called him darling. Joker felt the imprint of her small firm breast against his shoulder. Dammit. He'd hoped that she was just holding onto her skating as some kind of shield against the onslaught of emotions he'd stirred up in her. She was afraid to let herself respond to a man whose interest in her wasn't tied to her skating.

"What were you doing up in that tree anyhow?" Allison planted a soft kiss on his lips and smiled at him. "Tell me the truth."

"The top of the tree was dead and needed to be cut. And I needed to work out some of my . . . my frustrations with tough physical labor. I guess you wouldn't know about that kind of frustration, would you?"

"About frustration? Maybe not before, but I'm learning about a lot of new things, Joker. And frustration is pretty high on the list, along with anxiety, anger, and . . . desire. What can I do about mine?" Allison asked, allowing a hint of dispair to color her voice. "I don't suppose you have any ideas."

"I don't know what you mean," he said in a pained voice. "I think I heard you say something about taking care of me. I feel a little strange." He moaned and covered his eyes with his forearm.

"Just as I thought," Sandi observed dryly, "he's had a lick on the head. It's making him act crazy. I think we ought to take him down to the springs and dump him in—head first."

"Go away, Sandi," Joker said weakly. "I'll be perfectly all right by tomorrow morning. I have someone to look after me . . ." Joker's voice trailed off. He knew that he was making a mistake, allowing himself to respond to Allison's concern. But he couldn't hide his eagerness.

"All right, Jamie, no hospital," Allison said. "Don't worry, turnabout is fair play. I'll watch over you."

"Thank you. I think you're supposed to preven

people with head injuries from sleeping. Isn't that right, Sandi? Will you keep me awake, Beauty?"

"Of course." He was beginning to look better. When she'd seen his face smeared with blood, she'd been ready to panic. She hadn't realized how much she cared about the big guy until he'd passed out at her feet. Allison didn't want another minute of misunderstanding between them. She had to tell him the truth.

"About Mark," she began. "I have to tell you. I didn't mean it the way you thought. I don't care about Mark any more. Honest, I don't."

"Well," Sandi said with a nod of exasperation. "Here we go again. I guess neither of you wants any blueberry pancakes now."

When nobody answered, Sandi lifted her shoulders in resignation. "In that case, I'll just slide this batter in the refrigerator and skedaddle on out of here, while you two . . . do whatever it is that's going to keep Joker awake."

"Oh, but Sandi, I don't have any medical training. I don't have any idea what to do to keep Joker awake."

"I'm sure that you'll think of something."

The door slammed. They were alone. Joker rubbed his head, grimacing at the painful knot swelling above his right eye, and they stared at each other, each unwilling to speak, each unable to find the words.

"Jamie, I sorry I—" Allison said finally.

"Allison, I'm not ready—"

"You first," she broke in.

"No, I'm sorry. You go ahead."

"All right." Allison licked her lips and swallowed hard as she stared intently at the floor. "I didn't mean what I said the other night after we . . . I mean I wasn't even talking to you when I said that all I wanted was to skate. That's what I wanted when I came back here, but now I don't know what I want."

"Stop! Don't say another word." Joker slid off Allison's lap and came to his feet, lifting Allison in his arms. "I'm too heavy to be leaning on you. Let's sit in the swing while we talk. That is if you'll promise not to throttle me again. My head won't take the punishment."

"Put me down. You've just fallen out of a tree. You ought to take it easy."

"If you think I can stay there on the floor with you and take it easy, you're the one with the head injury. We're going to talk about this before either of us gets any more wild ideas."

"Fine, but I'll walk."

"No, I'll carry you."

"Jamie Daniel, you put me down, or I start screaming."

"Oh, by all means scream. And I'll scream louder."

"Joker, you wouldn't dare. What I ought to do now is lock you in the carriage house until you take this seriously. You could be badly hurt."

"But I'm not."

"Are you sure?"

"I'm sure."

"Then will you do something for me?"

"Of course I will, Beauty. Anything you say."

"Kiss me."

He kissed her.

"Oh, Joker, I thought I was going to have to find my own tree to climb."

Joker carried Allison out to the porch and sat down with her in his lap.

"We don't need trees, Beauty. We need each other. Our bodies understand that even if our minds don't. Our lips and arms are crazy about each other. And the rest of us isn't exactly playing hard to get."

He was right. She was already beginning to respond to his touch. Her body seemed to take a deep sigh of contentment and mold itself to the man.

"I don't understand you, Jamie Daniel. I'm tired and worn out, and I only have one good leg. What are you, some kind of nut? You can't really want me. It doesn't make any sense."

"Guess not," he agreed matter-of-factly, and shot a baleful look at her.

She leaned back and peered at Joker with eyes filled with bewilderment. She shook her head and tried once more. "Be serious, Joker. You deserve so much more."

"Maybe, but you're what I want, Allison." He tightened his grip on her body. The tension in her was almost visible. "Why don't we stop fighting each other and give ourselves a chance? What do we have to lose?"

"I'm afraid, Jamie," she whispered, feeling the ever-present stir of excitement begin to burn brighter. He was touching her, and that was all it took. Like a chain reaction, the tension began to ease.

"So am I. But I'm not going to hurt you, Beauty. I promise."

"I know. And I want to walk again, more than anything, but . . . well, it's wrong for me to take advantage of you," she said desperately, allowing her voice to trail off.

"And I told you, Allison Josey, that I was going to show you how wrong you are about yourself. I thought that night had proven it. I guess I have to do better."

"Oh, Jamie, thank you. But I am what I am, and I'm going to have to learn to accept the fact that I'll never skate again, and we both know that nobody will ever chase you with a shotgun on my behalf."

"Too bad, Allie. I might be able to look forward to that."

"Don't called me Allie," she said instinctively, and Joker felt the tension return like a blast of arctic air.

"Sorry, darling, is that what he called you?"

"Yes! Oh, Jamie, I'm sorry. It's just that Mark and I were together for so long. He was like a part of me, a part of me that's been cut away. I never had to function alone." Shyly, she clasped her hands behind Joker's head and leaned against his strong chest.

"I hate to hear you talk about him, but I know you have to work through that in order to heal and forget. I guess what I'm saying is that we need to move slowly. If we have something to offer each other, it ought to be given honestly, without expectations or guilt." He kissed her eyes shut and moved his hand to gently hold her cheek.

"I'm not sure that I understand, Jamie. I thought that I needed to be alone to get myself together. But being without you was awful. I like being close to you, having you kiss me. I even like having you glare at me in the exercise room. You know why?"

"Nope. Tell me."

"Because when you push me to try it one more time, it's because you want me to regain the use of my knee—for me."

"No, Beauty, it's for me. If you stay with me, it has

to be because you want to, not because you can't leave."

After a time Joker pushed the swing and it moved slowly back and forth, creaking comfortably in the silence. Soon he felt her begin to relax. Neither of them spoke as the sun filtered through the trees making lacy patterns across the patio floor.

"You may be right, Joker. I need to get well first. But can't I love you and want to skate too?"

"I don't know. I guess we'll have to see what you want. What we have to do now is get you walking again. After that, my Beauty, you can decide. Until then, I think you should look on my loving you as part of your therapy."

"Ah, Joker," she finally whispered sleepily, "what am I going to do with you?"

"Simple," he answered, pulling her closer, "you're going to love me back."

Nine

"You're in love with Allison? Good. I approve."

Mrs. Josey was sitting up in the rocking chair by the window. She was improving as rapidly as Allison. Soon she would be walking, and she could move into the apartment section of the nursing home.

"It would be good if she were really in love with me. But I'm all mixed up in her mind with skating again and with her sense of independence. She's an ice skater, a champion, and the last time I looked Pretty Springs was still in Georgia, and there isn't a big demand for ice skaters here. Once she's well, she'll go back. I can't let myself love her."

"But you do."

The time had come for honest answers. Joker took a deep breath and faced the question head on. "Yes. From the moment I saw her pictures on the study wall. But I didn't know it until she came to the gazebo that morning."

"And she loves you, too, Joker."

"What she feels for me is simply gratitude. I promised her I'd help her skate again, and she believes in me. She'd be unhappy without her career, and I wouldn't do that to her."

"What do you want from me, Joker?"

"Just your understanding, I suppose. I'd marry Allison tomorrow, but I want her to be able to skate again before she makes a decision. She has to be sure that she's over—that she wants me. Then we'll work it out somehow. But I'll never marry her knowing that she might come to resent me."

"Be careful, Joker. You might be the one to get hurt."

He might be the one to get hurt. There was nothing new about that. He'd had plenty of experience with his mother, Pop, Ellen. Oh, yes. He knew how much love could hurt. He'd never intended to let that happen again. Then he'd found Elysium, and he hadn't been able to stop himself from falling in love with a woman who was still hung up on another man.

Be careful, Joker. Mrs. Josey's words stayed with him all the way back to the estate. Careful was the one thing he hadn't been. And there was no way he could stop making love to Allison. He was binding her to him, and that wasn't fair. The hurting would be too hard when she left, on both of them. He drove around, considering what was best for Allison.

After long deliberation, he decided that no matter how painful it was, he'd do better to stay away from Allison unless other people were around. He'd let Sandi supervise the therapy program. He'd have the other therapists from the center come in and fill out the day. At night he'd invite Kaylyn and King over.

Hell, he'd even invite some of the patients from the nursing home to go with them to the springs. He'd keep her so busy that she'd fall asleep at night before she realized that he wasn't there. Somehow he'd keep his hands off her until she was well. Somehow.

The sun room had been equipped with stainless steel massage tables, complicated pulleys, bars, and machines. One half of the room held a Jacuzzi and a heated water bed.

When the phone rang, Joker answered it. When the postman came, Joker took the mail. When lunchtime came, he ate with her, enticing her to take just another bite, foisting vitamins and terrible-tasting concoctions on her, and gradually, Allison's body began to respond.

Joker was constantly in and out of the room, watching Allison as she went through the torture of the routines that had been prescribed, encouraging her with only a glance or a look that promised her reward after the day's schedule was complete. And every night Joker took her to the mineral springs, touching her knee, infusing her painful joint with the special glow of his hands.

Her progress seemed to accelerate at a frantic pace. But his plan to make sure they were never alone fell apart the first week. He couldn't stay away from her. It was as though everybody conspired to throw them together. In desperation he arranged for Sandi to stay at the house, and he manufactured excuses to be away at night, knowing that he was hurting Allison with his distance.

Allison, comfortable on her crutches now, was ready

to walk again, and it was Joker who forced her to accomplish it. His presence aggravated her, aggravated and stimulated her. He seemed consumed by the desire to make it possible for her to skate again, long after she'd decided that she'd be satisfied just to walk. And little by little she realized that he seemed more obsessed about her progress than she was. The only future he alluded to was one in which she was able to return to the ice.

By the next week Allison was so uptight that she wished Joker would spend his daytime hours in China. By the following week Allison wished *she* was in China. Was it anger, determination to show Joker that compelled her? She didn't know. She only knew that slowly and surely she began to walk without pain. Her bruised and battered knee was beginning to heal.

It was the rest of her body that seemed to be coming unglued. She couldn't sleep. Her appetite dwindled to nothing, and she had to force herself to go through the accelerated pace being demanded of her. Eventually her condition began to regress.

"What's wrong, Allison?" Sandi Arnold was standing behind her in the doorway to the gazebo.

"Wrong? Why, what could be wrong? Just look at the gardens. Joker has them almost totally restored. I can walk without my crutches. I actually bent my knee without pain last night in the springs. Everything is just peachy!"

"I'm not talking about your knee. I'm talking about you. You're wound as tight as a propeller on a toy airplane. One wrong move, and you're going to fly off into orbit."

"I'm fine, honest I am, Sandi. It's just that I'm

worried about what I'm going to do next. I mean, I didn't believe it when we started, but before long I'll be able to do the cancan." She managed a weak little laugh. "Do you know where an ex-ice skater can get a job as a cancan dancer?"

"It's Joker, isn't it? What's happened between you two? I saw the sparks fly between King and Kaylyn the moment they met, and the day that Joker fell out of that tree I saw it happening again. I thought you two were serious. What's wrong?"

Allison straightened her shoulders and jutted out her chin. "Oh, Sandi. I thought so too. But Joker seems to have changed his mind. I don't think he wants me anymore."

"Oh, I don't know. I just ran into Joker in the courtyard, and when I asked him if there was something he wanted, he growled at me as if he were a grizzly bear. I could understand about 'fool women who torture a man to death and ask dumb questions,' but the part about 'independence and mirrors of the soul' just sailed over my head."

"Independence?" And then it hit her full force. The idiot, the big, beautiful idiot. She was falling in love with him, but he refused to allow her to do that *because* he loved her. He was giving her the most important gift he could offer, her independence. Loving had been easy. Not loving was hard.

"I don't know what's happening between you two," Sandi observed dryly, "but I think the rest of us will be glad when you make up so that we can focus on your program."

"Oh? Well, this program has just had a change of focus. He thinks he can be noble and give me back my future without giving me any choice in the matter.

Well, we'll see about that." Allison pushed herself to her feet and strode down the hall. Inside the study she switched on the light and began ripping her pictures from the wall, throwing them into the fireplace one after the other.

"What are you doing?" Sandi stood watching, her face furrowed into a frown.

"I'm giving my Beast a future—me."

"Well, cleaning house might be one way for you to get rid of your tension. But what about Joker?"

"Joker." Allison laughed bitterly. "I hope he gets so brittle that he breaks into a thousand little pieces. I hope he finds himself a forest to chop down. Because I'm going to torture him to death—as soon as I figure out how to do it."

Sandi leaned against the door frame and pursed her lips as if she were calculating the dimensions of the rug. "Oh, I don't know, Allison. If there was something I really wanted, I think I could figure out a way to get it. Women are pretty devious when they want to be."

"But if you have to be devious to get what you want, how can you be sure that you can keep it?"

"Allison, honey, if Joker's your problem, I'm dead sure that you're his. He's moved heaven and earth to help you recover. Maybe it's time for you to give something back to him. Even if he doesn't think he ought to have it."

"But, Sandi," Allison admitted listlessly, "I've tried everything I know. I don't know how to . . ."

"Horsefeathers! All women know how to, we just don't let the men know that we do. We're finished here for the day. I think you'll find that everybody is going to be busy tonight when you get to the springs. Do you think you and Joker can manage alone?"

"Yes," she said softly. "I'll manage. I'll do it, one way or another."

The Sports Medicine Rehabilitation Center was deserted. There was no other vehicle in the parking area, and the lights inside the lobby were off.

"Wonder where everybody is?" Joker asked uneasily. Allison had been behaving strangely ever since he'd picked her up at the house. There'd been a kind of contained excitement about her that he hadn't seen before.

"All Sandi said was that they'd meet us here," Allison answered vaguely, and walked through the lobby toward the rock-walled room where the springs bubbled to the surface.

"Well, you go on and get undressed. I'll wait for Sandi."

"Fine," Allison answered, casually disappearing into the darkness. "But you ought to find a suit, in case something happens and she doesn't show up."

Allison bit back a smile. Sandi had been right. She could be devious if she wanted to be. And she'd decided beyond a shadow of a doubt that she wanted Joker. It had taken her a long time to figure out his plan to give her her independence, and she loved him for it. She loved the big adorable lug. Her decision to make love to him was a measure of her new independence.

In the recessed light from the edge of the pool, Allison slipped her terry cloth robe from her body and stood by the water, completely still, completely nude. She felt the mist shower her skin with droplets of heated water.

"Joker?"

"Yes?" His voice sounded a long way off as it echoed around the room.

"Joker, would you come in here, please? I . . . I need you."

Joker groaned. The last thing he wanted to do was to go into that room alone with Allison. For weeks he'd paced the edge of the rocks and watched her go through a series of exercises under the careful supervision of one person or another. He'd massaged her knee, held it in his big hands with as much control as he could muster, never giving in to the need to slide those hands up her body, to touch her breasts, to kiss her. He didn't know how much longer he'd be able to hold out. And now they were alone, the one thing he'd avoided.

"Joker, please. I'm waiting."

"Hell! Allison, what do you need?" He pushed aside his fears, strode into the spring room, and swallowed his last rational breath of air.

"You, Jamie. I need you."

She was standing across the room beside the springs. She was totally nude. The muted light bathed her in blue and lavender, creating a kind of halo around her. No longer thin, no longer awkward, she stood with her arms outstretched like some Grecian siren calling to her lover god.

"Ah, Beauty," his voice dropped to a husky pitch, "why are you doing this to me?"

"I love you, you sweet man. And I need you to love me." Boldly she put her hands on her breasts and caressed them, bringing them to tight hard peaks of desire. "I'm going crazy wanting you, Jamie." She started toward him.

She was in his arms, and he hadn't known that he'd moved. His kiss was savage and hard, and she returned it, giving as much as she got. And then his clothes were gone, and they were wound together, bare skin to bare skin. His tongue delved into her mouth as though he were dying and she were his only chance to live.

He pulled his lips away. "Lord, I've missed touching you." With one hand he lifted her so that he could take her nipple inside his mouth. He heard her soft cry of desire as she arched herself against him.

Joker's other hand slid down between them, touching the throbbing softness between her legs. "I've missed touching you here. Is this what you want from me, Beauty?"

Allison couldn't speak. She could only give in to the delicious waves of sensations his fingers evoked. "Oh, Jamie, why? Why did you go away from me?"

"I had to. You said that you didn't want to depend on another man. I knew you still cared about Mark. I didn't want you to feel that way about me. You had to walk without crutches—by yourself."

"Watch this, Jamie. Here, let me show you. Stand back." She pulled herself out of his arms, took several steps away, whirled around triumphantly, and danced back again. "See?"

"Yes, that's great, Beauty. I'm happy for you."

"What's wrong, Jamie, did I do something wrong?" She pushed herself against him, placing her hand on either side of his face and pulling him down so that she could plant slow, erotic kisses across his mouth and down his chest.

"No. You haven't done anything wrong."

"Don't you want me anymore, Jamie?" Her heart tightened until she heard his anguished groan.

"Want you? Ah, Beauty, you're all I want. I can't turn away from you again." He glanced around at the short benches and hard rock floor, then lifted her until she straddled his body as he walked down into the bubbling water.

Hungrily he kissed her, ravishing her mouth, plunging his tongue in and out with such intensity that she felt as if she were about to explode. And then he lifted her and brought her down on his rigid sex, thrusting into her until she clasped her legs around his body and held him tightly inside her.

Joker went suddenly still. He looked down at Allison, into her passion-filled eyes, at the sudden undeniable knowledge that she wanted him, truly wanted him enough to trick him into taking her. His kiss softened, and he knew in that moment, without any doubt, that he truly loved her—and would for all time.

When he began to move her up and down against him again, he felt the warmth of his touch flood over both of them. They clung to each other as the heat began to build. He couldn't hold back any longer. He didn't have to. As he emptied himself into her, he felt the unmistakable contractions of her body, and they both were consumed by the passion of their release.

"I hope you can walk, Jamie. I don't think I can," Allison said quite a while later.

"Ah, Beauty, why did you do this?" He continued to stand, still holding her, unwilling to separate himself from her.

"Why did you go away from me, Jamie?"

"I didn't want to leave you, Beauty. I just knew that you needed to heal. It was wrong of me to play on your physical needs. I had to stay away, or you'd become dependent on me."

"Jamie Daniel, you fool, I'm in love with you. I never knew what that meant before. I want you in my bed. I want you inside me tonight and tomorrow night and every night after that. I'm going to become very dependent on at least one part of you. Let's go home, darling—and hurry."

He did. The next morning he visited the local drug store. Allison might think that she couldn't conceive, but Joker had the feeling that she was wrong. They were courting disaster, and if by some stretch of heaven's good wishes he was able to keep her, he didn't want her decision to be for any other reason than love. That afternoon they had the bed in the carriage house moved into the master bedroom, and the water bed in the sun room became obsolete.

The garden bloomed. The sun shone in colors more vivid than ever before. Joker closed his eyes to the future. He'd given all he had to give—himself. He didn't want to know what would happen when Allison was well enough to leave him. He could only love her, silently and completely. And wait for their time to end.

Ten

"So you're Lillian? Are all of you so different?"

"Yep, when Pop dealt this hand, he really scrambled the cards. King is the damn-the-torpedoes, full-speed-ahead type. Jack's the silent, still-waters-run-deep kind. And Joker's the wild card."

"And you're like Jamie. I think I would have known you were Jamie's sister even if you hadn't told me."

"Jamie?" The dark-haired woman gave a warm laugh and clapped her hands in delight. "I can see how you did it. He didn't have a chance."

"Oh, but he did. He could have let me fall into the moat with the crocodiles."

"Oh, my. I'm sorry I stayed out of this. It must have been great fun. You made him fall out of a tree and hit his head?" Diamond doubled up in a fresh attack of laughter.

Allison was sitting in the kitchen at the breakfast table with Diamond Vandergriff, the sophisticated beauty who was Joker's sister. Diamond had rung her doorbell only moments after Joker had left to check on his landscaping job at the new office complex. Any worries Allison might have had over being friends with her future sister-in-law vanished the moment Diamond slipped off her high-heeled shoes and padded in her stocking feet into the kitchen, sniffing the tantalizing aroma of the peach pie that Minnie had brought by earlier.

Now, two cups of coffee and a wedge of pie later, Diamond was asking questions that Allison might have felt were too personal to answer coming from anyone else.

"And you didn't know that Joker was really James Daniel Vandergriff?"

"No, I thought he was a yard man my grandmother took in, a gardener who gambled on the side."

"So," Diamond prodded, "you two fell in love. You've regained the use of your knee, and Joker's going back to work. So, when's the wedding?"

"That's the problem. Joker thinks that what I feel for him is only gratitude, and because we're . . ." Allison let her voice trail off. She couldn't tell Joker's sister that her brother thought she was grateful to him because their lovemaking was so wonderful. But that was one of the things he believed. He was right. Making love with Joker was wonderful, but what she felt for him was much more.

They both loved Elysium. They both loved her grandmother, and they'd both managed to hide their vulnerability. She'd put all her energy into creating a fantasy on ice, and Joker had lived in a world he'd created for himself.

"We haven't talked about marriage. I can't seem to make the big lug understand that I love him."

"Knowing Joker, I can buy that. He's got some crazy idea that love equals loss. So if he doesn't love you back, he won't lose you. He'd rather think that you're suffering from a case of gratitude. What excuse does he give you?"

"He thinks he's giving me my independence. The real truth is that he needs me to need him. And he thinks I won't, after I'm well. I don't think he's ever loved a woman before, though." Allison dropped her head shyly as she spoke. "I know he is very experienced."

"So, he thinks that you're in love with him because you're grateful, and you think that he's in love with you because of some need to be needed. Balderdash!"

"What?" Allison watched Diamond come to her feet and pace back and forth, rubbing her forefinger against her chin in thought as she paced.

"It seems to me, my future sister-in-law, that what we have here is two people full of guilt. They've got a good thing, and they can't enjoy it for feeling guilty over getting the most out of the relationship."

"You may be right," Allison admitted. "I'm certainly no stranger to guilt. Everything has always come to me. This house, Gran, skating, the gold medal. And now Joker. Maybe I don't deserve it."

"Crimeny! We have two guilty bleeding hearts here. Joker's gone through life making everything easy for everybody else—his landlady, his teachers, the rest of his family—he's always been the caretaker. He's still giving—giving you a way out. Noble jackass."

"Now wait a minute. Granted, he may be too giving, but there isn't a more wonderful, caring, exciting man in the world. He's taught me about love. He just won't let me love him back."

"And that, Allison Josey, is the heart of the problem. He's taught you how to give. Now, you're going to have to teach him how to take. He's never learned that. If I were you," Diamond said shaking her head in mock despair, "I'd fill up that moat, starve out the crocs, and let up the drawbridge until you figure out a way to convince Joker that you don't want to go back to your skating career. Otherwise, I think he'll probably rent a rink for you to start practicing on."

Allison walked Diamond to the door. "Thank you, Lillie," Allison said, planting a kiss on her cheek. "Maybe I've been going about this all wrong. I think maybe I'll have to work out a new routine."

"As in skating?"

"Sure, a new move, new costume, change my style. Yep, there's more than one way to take the prize."

Diamond gave Allison an encouraging hug. "Is there anything I can do to help?"

"I don't think so, unless you know where I can buy some live chickens."

"Chickens? Don't try and explain. This is going to be a marriage made in heaven," Diamond said with a smile.

After her future sister-in-law left, Allison giggled out loud as she planned how she'd prove herself to her reluctant fiancé. Finding the chickens was first on her list. The second thing she would do was learn how to cook. She hadn't been so excited since she'd tried out for the Olympic team.

Joker's singing voice didn't actually scare buzzards as he'd told Allison, but he did startle a fellow motorist or two on the way home with his mournful rendition of a country music song bemoaning the loss of his one true love. He'd done it. Weeks ago he'd invited Darron Vardin, the director of Allison's ice show, to the reception that King and Diamond were planning to kick off the publicity for the Sports Medicine Rehabilitation Center. Allison was almost ready to go back to work, he'd assured Darron, and she was being courted by the competition. Darron had agreed to come. He'd done it, he'd healed Allison's knee and given her back her career.

And he'd never been so miserable in his life.

When Joker reached the estate, he found a shiny new sign at the entranceway proclaiming this property as a part of the sovereign territory of Texas. Mulling over the significance of the psychedelic work of art, he rounded the curve in the driveway and was forced to come to a screeching halt in the midst of a flock of assorted chickens and roosters, who'd taken up residence in the courtyard.

Something very strange was going on.

Inside the house there was something even stranger happening. Great clouds of smoke were billowing from the kitchen. The house was on fire. Joker's breathing stopped as he charged into the smoke-filled room.

"Beauty! Where are you, Allison?"

"Oh, Joker, it's terrible!"

Allison, face smeared with soot, rushed into his arms and began to cry. "I've ruined it, totally and completely burned it to a crisp."

"Beauty, darling, what's burned to a crisp?" Joker lifted Allison into his arms and dashed out through the sun room to the garden.

"The roast. The lovely roast I was cooking for

dinner. Even the little paper hats I put on the ribs caught on fire and burned up." She hiccupped helplessly.

"You mean all that smoke is coming from a burned roast?"

"No, it's coming from the water I poured on the roast to put out the fire. Just look at me. After all my plans to surprise you, I'm a complete flop."

By this time Joker was looking. Allison's costume was as startling as the scene he'd been greeted with. She was wearing high-heeled satin shoes and white lacy stockings that attached to a garter belt beneath a soft pink see-through negligee. Over her calendar-art seduction costume, she'd tied the pink gingham apron he'd worn the first night she'd been at home.

"Failure? Lawdy, Miss Claudie, if I'm going to be welcomed by this every night, who wants success?"

Two chickens suddenly squawked wildly and began a mad dash through the garden.

"Beauty, I love holding you like this, but I have to know. What in hell are you doing?"

"Oh, Jamie, I wanted to show you that being married to me would be exciting. Gran is going to teach me to cook. And I thought if you stopped seeing me as a skater and started seeing me as a real woman, you'd want to marry me."

"And that's why you're turning this place into a chicken coop?"

"Well, in the movie they called it a chicken ranch. I just wanted to . . . seduce you. Will you teach me to do the Texas two-step, Jamie?"

He looked down at her soot-smeared face and laughed out loud. "All this is to make me want to marry you? Oh, Beauty, there hasn't been one minute since I first saw your picture hanging on that study wall that I haven't wanted you."

"But that was Allison the skater. This is Allison the woman. What about it, big boy, wanna make this the first day of the rest of our lives?" She lowered one eyelash and gave an exaggerated wink as she ran her fingertips around his neck and pulled his head down to meet her kiss.

"Day, hell," Joker finally managed to growl. "I'd rather start with the night."

He turned and started up the steps to the carriage house. "Are you sure the fire is out back there?"

"I'm sure, you big lug. The only fire you have to put out is the one right here."

And he did, magnificently and efficiently, carefully attending to any hot spots that flared up in the night.

The next few days were the most wonderful time of Allison's life. She and Joker made glorious love in the springs, in the bedroom, and once in the gazebo. One night Joker produced a pair of big thick white athletic socks and some old rock and roll records. They had their own version of a sock hop, which soon disintegrated into an entirely new concept of where the sock should be placed.

As she fell deeper and deeper in love, there were times when Allison was sure that Joker trusted the love she'd pledged to him. Then she'd see him gaze off into the distance as a pained look flashed in his eyes. She knew he'd always played the clown to cover the hurt he'd felt at the loss of his parents and the hard life he and his siblings had had to lead to exist without them. He still didn't trust in their love.

One night they joined King and Kaylyn and Diamond at the Waterhole. But it was King who gave the final stamp of approval, when he saw Allison and Joker together.

"You're damned lucky, brother. A man doesn't often find such a woman."

"I hope that you're going to make an honest woman out of her, James Daniel," Diamond teased.

"I think I'm going to have to talk with Chief Newton personally," Allison quipped. "Do you know if he has a shotgun?"

"Poor Allison," Kaylyn said sadly, "she's being taken advantage of by a rogue."

"Why poor Allison?" Joker interjected. "Take pity on poor Joker. His home has been turned into a chicken ranch."

The light banter went on all evening. But nobody was more aware than Allison, that Joker never gave a real answer to their teasing questions.

They were in the big bedroom, lights on, clothes falling like moon shadows on the carpet. Joker took her in his arms and made sweet, poignant love to her, bringing them to new heights of desire.

"You have a lot of friends, don't you, Jamie? Have you ever met anybody you didn't like?" She was lying in Joker's arms, at peace with the world.

"Not lately. The world seems to have greatly improved since I met you, Allison."

"It isn't the world, Jamie Daniel, it's you and those enchanted eyes you view the world with. You've made me see through them too."

"Well, you'd better close your enchanted eyes," Joker

said, kissing each one with loving care. "It's very late. Tomorrow I think I'll give you a little vacation. I have some family business I have to take care of."

"Good, I'll take another cooking lesson."

"Just as long as you don't have any more of those little paper hats."

"Ah, shucks, I thought I might visit the local gourmet store and do a little personal shopping. If I'm going to cook, I need a professional chef's apron and cap, don't you think?"

"Maybe you'd like me to take your measurements. Now that sounds like my kind of kitchen duty."

He was right, and she liked it very much.

Allison headed off Sandi Arnold when she came the next morning for a therapy session.

"Sandi, would you have time to take me down to the Sports Medicine Center this morning? I'd like to talk to the doctor. There is a medical director on the staff, isn't there?"

"Sure. That'll be great. I've been trying to get you down to see him for weeks. Let me give him a call and tell him we're on our way. Isn't Joker coming too?"

"No. He has work to do today. So I'm going to surprise him and get an official medical evaluation."

In less than half an hour Allison had changed her clothes, and they were on their way. She tried to pretend that she wasn't nervous, but she hadn't been so anxious since she'd made the first trip to the nursing home to see Gran. She knew her knee was vastly improved, but she couldn't be certain how much was real and how much was Joker's magic.

"What made you change your mind?" Sandi asked as she turned into the parking area.

"Let's just say that I've got a yen to go shopping."

"Well, the last time I looked there weren't any shops in the center."

"Nope, but there's a doctor who ought to be able to tell me for sure how soon I'll be able to walk down the aisle."

"Well, pardon me. But I'd say that you're capable of that now. What me to come in with you?"

"Nope, I'll manage. I'm an independent lady, or haven't you noticed?"

Allison gave Sandi a bright smile and slid out of the car. They agreed that Sandi would be back in an hour to pick her up and drive her back to the estate.

Inside, Allison was shown into the office of the doctor who'd been supervising her program all along. He agreed that her knee had responded beyond their wildest expectations, that her body had returned to normal, and that there was no physical reason that she shouldn't conceive a child if that was what she wanted.

Allison didn't feel the floor beneath her feet as she floated down the hall into the lobby. She heard the tinkling melody of the springs and felt her spirits soar. Through the glass doors she saw the lizard beaming in the sunlight. He was smiling. She was smiling. The handsome, sandy-haired man with the serious expression who was coming through the door caught sight of her and began to smile as well.

"Allison Josey?" He pulled a pair of horn-rimmed glasses from his face and held out his hand. "I'm Tom Brolin, editor of the *Gazette*. I'm so pleased to meet you at last."

A reporter. For a moment Allison's heart sank. *No, no more shrinking violet, Allison Josey. You're an independent woman now.*

"How do you do, Mr. Brolin. Isn't it a nice day?"

"Indeed. Please let me thank you. Your generosity is going to mean so much to the people of Pretty Springs. For a while there I thought the springs were going under. But you and Joker will make it all happen."

"Generosity? I'm not sure I understand. What have I done?"

"Don't be modest. Just look at you. You're a credit to the Vandergriffs' faith in the springs. Do you realize what your rehabilitation means to the local people?"

"I realize what it means to me," Allison responded brightly, thinking of wedding dresses and candlelit chapels.

"By endorsing the springs publicly, you'll bring in the national sports figures that we need. Your acting as spokesperson will literally save the springs. I can see the headlines now. FAMOUS OLYMPIC STAR LIVING TESTIMONY TO HEALING POWER OF PRETTY SPRINGS. Joker is a miracle worker."

"Testimony. You mean Joker had this in mind all the time? He expected me to—"

"Oh, yes. There was never a doubt in his mind that you'd be able to skate again. He said that all along. We owe him a debt of gratitude. King said he'd find a way to save the springs. He's done it before."

"Joker?" Allison felt her world crash at her feet. "You mean that by learning to skate again I'll be the local attraction at the springs? Me and the lizard? I guess he knew what he was doing, all right. Isn't that grand?"

"What's wrong?" Tom Brolin replaced his glasses on his nose and looked at Allison with concern. "Did I say something wrong? I know that Joker warned us that you wanted your privacy, but I thought now that you were practically well, you wouldn't be distressed. I assure you, I'm not taking any pictures or releasing any information until you're ready."

"Yes, well, that may be a very long time." Allison dashed past the puzzled man and darted down the steps and into Sandi's waiting car.

"What's wrong, Allison? Was the news bad?"

"It depends on your point of view, Sandi, where does a person stay in Pretty Springs if she's just going to be in town temporarily?" Allison crossed her arms over her chest and tried to control her urge to scream.

"Well, when I first came here, I stayed in the Pretty Springs Inn."

"Fine, take me there."

"Why? Are you moving out?"

"Exactly. I'd appreciate it if you'd take me home so I can pack my clothes."

"Come on, kid, you aren't going anywhere, are you? I mean, even if the news isn't good, Joker isn't going to give up. He's going to make you skate again, if it's the last thing he ever does."

"The way I feel right now, that may very well be true." She'd fallen for his line, knowing all the time that he was nothing but a wheeler-dealer. He'd never really intended to marry her.

Mark, Joker—they were all the same, using her for their own purposes. Neither one of them loved her. Oh, they'd made love to her, and she, foolish Allison, had believed that making love meant the same thing to Joker that it had to her. She'd been wrong again.

Allison and Sandi argued the entire time Allison packed her clothes.

"I don't guess you'd like to tell me what you're upset about, would you, Allison? This doesn't have anything to do with seeing the doctor, does it?"

"No! If you don't already know, ask the editor of the *Gazette*. Or ask Joker. He has all the answers. If he doesn't, he'll make up a few original ones."

They argued as Sandi drove Allison to the inn.

"Maybe we'd better wait for Joker and let you talk this over. If he comes home and you're gone, he won't understand, will he?"

"I think he'll understand very well," Allison said. "It just takes me a little longer to get the picture. His name is James Daniel Vandergriff. The Vandergriff family is the most important thing in Joker's world, and the Vandergriff family translates to Vandergriff, Inc. Yep, I finally understand."

Allison paid for a week's stay at the inn and moved in.

Sandi gave up arguing when she was finally convinced that Allison wasn't going back to the estate.

Once Sandi left, Allison continued the argument with herself. It was all very clear now. Joker had planned it from the beginning. He would rehabilitate an athlete—who better than Allison Josey, local girl who'd become world famous and had disappeared? Then he had planned to use her to publicize the Sports Medicine Rehabilitation Center so that it would be a success. Sure, he wanted her to skate again. How else could he use her as an example?

For nearly a week she expected Joker to come for her. She'd prepared herself for a confrontation, but when she opened the door five days later, it was King who stood there.

"May I come in?"

"Why? I don't think we have anything to talk about."

"I think we do. Joker doesn't believe that you'll listen to him, but maybe you'll listen to me. Joker vetoed the idea of having you endorse the springs the moment it came up. He doesn't blame you for thinking what you did. He should have told you about our problems. But Joker can't talk about personal trouble. He never could."

"Maybe, but your newspaper editor already has the front page pasted up. That sounds pretty definite to me."

"Everybody is involved in the grand opening reception. Tom just assumed when he saw you coming out of the doctor's office that you were there to discuss the plans. He's sorry. We're all sorry. We get carried away with the importance of the center. But we'd never ask you to do something you didn't feel comfortable with."

"It isn't just that. Why didn't Joker mention the idea to me? It should have been my decision, not his."

"He knew you'd feel obligated, and he didn't want to put any pressure on you. And by now you should know Joker. He never accepts anything unpleasant. He thought he'd come up with another way. For weeks he's been calling friends inviting them to the reception. He figured that if enough of them see Minnie and Luther, they'll give the springs a try. Otherwise, I don't know. I'm afraid that we may be in big trouble."

"Is he having any luck?"

"I don't know. Maybe. That's not important. If Vandergriff, Inc. has a few setbacks, we'll recover. We've done it before. The important thing is you and Joker. You belong together."

"Well, you'll have a hard time convincing him of that," Allison said, her voice full of pain. She'd been wrong. For the first time she'd fallen in love. Yet the first time she'd been called on to prove her devotion, she'd failed. She'd disappeared just like Mark. And she hadn't called either. At least Joker had never made promises he couldn't keep. He'd expected her to leave him—and she had.

"Allison, I know my brother. If Joker has to walk down Peachtree Street stark naked to protect you, he'll do it. Please, don't leave him. He's convinced that you'll go like everybody else he's ever cared for."

"Go like everyone else? Not on your life, King Vandergriff. If there's one thing your brother has taught me, it's that a person can do just about anything she really wants to. I'm going to endorse those springs. I'm going to find a way to bring the world to Pretty Springs, and, my brother-in-law-to-be, your brother's going to make an honest woman out of me—whether he wants to or not."

"Good luck, Allison. I think Joker's going to have a very interesting life."

"So do I. But I have to work fast. You're more right than you could possibly know."

•   •   •   •

A story in the Pretty Springs *Gazette* about the visit of the Summer Olympic Site Committee to Atlanta gave Allison the solution to the problem. The reception to honor the grand opening of the new Sports Medicine Rehabilitation Center at the Pretty Springs Golf and Tennis Retirement Community gave her the means to accomplish it.

By the next morning she was sitting in King Vandergriff's office with her proposal. By the next afternoon King gave her the approval of the board of directors and stockholders to carry out her plan.

The site committee for the Summer Olympics was already considering Atlanta as a possible site for the 1996 summer games. As a personal favor to Allison, they'd added a stop at the reception to their itinerary. Allison explained the healing properties of the springs, and at her suggestion her old coach agreed to present a proposal to consider the center as a rehabilitation site for the athletes. If one gold medal winner's endorsement would publicize the springs, a whole team's ought to be just perfect.

The results were out of her hands. She'd done all she could. She'd simply have to sit back and wait. In the meantime she'd go and share her plans with Gran.

"Allison, I can't possibly go to that reception in a wheelchair," Lenice Josey protested.

"Oh, yes you can. If I'm going to be on display, so are you. We'll show 'em, Gran." Allison laughed out loud. "Ah, Gran, I'm going husband-hunting, and I wouldn't want you to miss the fun."

"All right, if you're sure. But I've got to get my hair and my nails done. And I'll have Minnie take a tuck in my blue dinner gown. Oh, Allison, I can't wait to see Joker's face."

"There's no point in her old boss coming," Joker complained to his sister-in-law Kaylyn. "I only invited him so that he could see that Allison was ready to go back to work, and now she isn't even going to be at the reception."

"You never know how things are going to turn out, Joker. You go on into Atlanta and pick him up. Maybe the ice show contact will be profitable for the health center. Allison can't be the only skater who is injured."

"Maybe." Joker tugged at the collar of his tux and crawled into his van. What he'd have liked to do was dump Darron Vardin into the springs and go back to the gazebo and the first day Allison had stumbled into his arms. He'd been so sure that he'd done the right thing for her. But maybe he'd made a big mistake.

Allison felt that old threat of panic sweep over her as she began to dress. Ice shows and Olympic events were simple. A social occasion that forced her to meet her old friends and past associates would be difficult. Her Olympic coaches would be there. They all knew everything about her, and she still wasn't sure she could face the questions. But she had to do it—for Joker.

Who was she fooling? It was Joker she was afraid to face. What if she were wrong? What if he didn't really want her?

After a long soak in the tub, a long nap, and a pep talk from Diamond, she was ready to face him. She pinned her hair into a severe chignon, glanced in the mirror, and loosened several curls to drape softly around her face. She applied a dark coating of eye shadow and some mascara. Her skin was paler than usual, and she knew it was because she'd never before taken such a gamble with her future.

Over her shoulders she pulled her only long dress, a backless ebony gown that glimmered like stars when the light caught the sequins. There was a scandalous slit up the back that allowed her to walk. Adding a pair of diamond earrings, Allison slipped her feet into matching black heels. Her last move was to stick a pearl white chicken feather in the knot of hair at the base of her neck. To heck with fashion, she thought. She was making a statement to the man she loved.

Jack was obviously taken aback when he opened the door and saw the woman standing in the light. "Good evening, Allison. You're stunning. I'm not sure my brother deserves such a beautiful wife. Your grandmother is in the car."

"They are coming, aren't they?"

"If you mean the Olympic Site Committee, yes, they arrived a little after six. Diamond took them to dinner."

"And Joker?"

"Yes, he'll be there. You really love him, don't you?" Jack draped her wrap about her shoulders and escorted her to the big black Lincoln parked in the courtyard.

"I really do."

"You two are something," Jack observed, shaking

his head in disbelief. "I just hope your plans don't backfire and you both end up losing the game."

"Both? Oh, Jack, what is Joker up to? Is he still trying to get rid of me?"

"Well, let's say that he's going to make it easy for you to be gone." Jack started the engine. "We'd better hurry. King has the reception under control, but we don't want to be late."

The crowd was worse than she'd imagined. The entire population of Pretty Springs had been invited to tour the center between six and eight. Now the VIP group was arriving. From the moment Allison walked into the hall, she was overwhelmed by old friends.

"Hi, Allison, you look great." The speaker was vaguely familiar, but no name came to mind. "We're glad you're back," called another.

"That's wonderful. Thank you." Allison moved away to speak to the next group, pushing Gran through the crowd until Sandi Arnold intercepted them and took Mrs. Josey over to join Minnie and Luther Peavey by the speaker's stand.

The Olympic Site Committee was easy to identify when they arrived. They were wearing matching red jackets with blue vests. Photographers and reporters mobbed the committee members, peppering them with questions about their opinions of Atlanta's chances to be the site for the 1996 summer games. The officials had already been taken on a tour of the facilities, and now they fanned out, eager to discuss the power of the springs.

Allison made herself available to the committee, giving her own testimony as to the success of the healing water. As she spoke her gaze continually swept the crowd. He had to be there. Jack had told her that he was coming. But so far she'd seen no sign of red hair or a bushy beard.

"I can't believe how well you look," one of the committee members observed. "I heard about what happened. I thought that you weren't expected to walk again."

"It's the springs," Allison answered positively, "the miracle healing springs, along with the man I'm going to marry, whose magical hands brought me back completely after I'd been given up on as a lost cause. This is what I want to share with all of you. That's why I asked the committee to tour our facilities and hear what we have to offer."

And then she saw Darron Vardin, the man who'd been the creative director of the Carnival Ice Follies. He was the last person she'd ever expected to see, and he was headed straight for her.

"Hello, Allison. You look great."

"How nice to see you, Darron. What are you doing here?"

"Looking for you. Someone told me you'd be here and that you were ready to go back to work. What about it, sugar, want to give the ice another whirl?"

"You're offering me a job?" It was incredible. Jack had hinted that Joker was up to something, but this was the one thing she'd never expected to happen. He'd promised her that she would skate again, and he'd given her a second chance at a career. "No, thanks."

Darron looked surprised. "Why not, Allie? Not many people get a second chance."

"You don't know how right you are," Allison said,

fervently searching the crowd for the big titian-haired man with the beard.

"So the answer is no. Why?"

"Simple. I want to skate again, and I probably will. But I've found something I want more. Oh!"

She'd been looking at him for several minutes before she recognized him. Joker was wearing a tuxedo. Standing with Tom Brolin, he was watching her.

At that distance she felt Joker's touch, and her skin rippled in response. No wonder she hadn't recognized him. He'd shaved his beard and mustache. No longer was he a burly, bushy-haired giant. He was an imposing, sophisticated, debonair executive. Gone was the mustache that had fired her lips with its touch. Gone was the beard that caressed her breasts with fire. He was breathtakingly handsome, and suddenly she wasn't certain that she could carry out her plan. What in heaven's name would a man like that want with a woman like her?

"I'm sorry, Darron. Thank you, but you've made a trip here for nothing. I'm not coming back to the show, now or ever."

"What about Mark?" His casual words stopped her, but only for a moment.

"What do you mean, what about Mark?"

"He's completed his tour in Europe. He wants to see you, Allison. We thought you two might get back together again. Think what a splash you'd make."

Mark was coming back? At one time she would have given anything to hear that. He wanted her back. The thought evaporated almost as soon as it came to mind. All she wanted now was to get the man she loved.

"Tell him that I wish him good luck, but I can't accept your offer. I have other plans, that is if a certain rogue has any intention of doing the proper thing. You don't by any chance have a shotgun, do you?"

"Shotgun?" She left Darron mulling over her strange refusal as she threaded her way across the room.

"Friends, distinguished guests, and members of the press," King Vandergriff said as he stepped before the podium. "On behalf of the entire Vandergriff family and the board of directors, I'm delighted that you could join us to celebrate the grand opening of the Pretty Springs Sports Medicine Rehabilitation Complex here at our Golf and Tennis Retirement Community. And I am pleased to make a special announcement. Pending approval by the governing board, we have been tentatively selected as the official rehabilitation center for the members of our U.S. Olympic Team for the next four years."

An "oooooh" went up from the crowd.

"And"—King clapped his hands to regain control —"I'd also like to announce that our own Olympic gold medalist, Allison Josey, has agreed to accept the position as director of our program and liaison officer between the Olympic Committee and our sports medicine staff. Would you please come to the platform, Allison? I'm sure that the press would like a picture of you and your fiancé and the chairman of the Olympic Site Committee shaking hands on the agreement."

Allison reached Joker's side and looked up at the stunned man with a smile. "Is it all right, big guy? Do you have any objection to your wife working?"

"But your skating," he whispered dazedly. "Won't you miss it?"

"Probably, but I expect to be very busy with . . . lots of new things. Please, Joker, touch me. I need you. I'm scared to death to go up there alone."

"You want me to come with you?"

She grinned at his choice of words. "Always, Jamie. I need you with me always." She tugged at his arm and pulled him along to the platform, posing for pictures and smiling with happiness that would never be artificial as long as his hand was touching her.

After obliging the press with answers to their questions, Allison told her friends good-bye, gave her grandmother a big wink, slid her hand into the crook of Joker's arm, and carefully maneuvered him through the crowd and out the door.

"Why, Allison?" Joker pulled her into the shadow of Lizard Rock, the great guardian of the healing springs that gave the city its name. "I saw you talking to Darron Vardin. I knew he was offering you your old job back."

"Uh-huh! How do you suppose he came to be here?" She looped her arms around his waist and looked up at him in the moonlight, this clean-shaven stranger who looked as if he had stepped off the pages of a magazine.

"I . . . I called him," Joker answered. "How'd those Olympic people get here?"

"I . . . called them," Allison shifted her body, pressing herself suggestively against her beautiful protector.

"But you wanted to skate again. You should," Joker argued, feeling the familiar rise of heat in his body where they touched.

"Uh-huh." She slid her fingertips up his backbone, counting each vertebra until she reached the back of his neck.

"Why did you do it, Beauty?"

"I love you, Jamie Daniel. You need me as much as I need you. I finally figured it out. It wasn't being a star that made me want to skate again, it was belonging. And I found the place where I belong. I never loved Mark. He's in the past, and I've put that behind me. You let me prove to myself that I can run my own life, and I'm doing exactly what I want to do.

"And when you clowned around and used your special touch, you were just trying to make yourself belong too. And where we both want to be is right here, with each other. You need me to love you, James Daniel Vandergriff."

"I do?"

"You do. And I'm not going anywhere. We are getting married two weeks from Sunday. The arrangements are already made."

"They are?"

"They are. This is one decision that I intend to see carried out."

"Yes, ma'am. I wouldn't dream of trying to tell somebody else what to do."

"And you're going to let your beard grow back right away."

"You don't like me as a handsome prince?"

"Nope, I want my beast back."

"Yes, ma'am." His answer was meek enough. But the wicked glint in his eye gave her the true picture of what she could expect when they got back to Elysium.

"I never told you that I love you, Allison."

"Yes, you did, Jamie, every time you carried me in your arms, every time you did some foolish wonderful thing to help me walk, every time you kissed me. You told me."

"And you're sure you want to give up everything for a simple gardener who likes to make things grow?"

"No, I'm not giving up anything, you wonderful man. And making things grow is exactly what I have in mind. I want to have a child right away. Will you give me a child, Jamie?"

"I'll give you anything you want. You've made me so very happy, my darling. I have things to give you that you don't even suspect. Let's go home."

When Joker carried her to the van, she didn't argue. The aura of his touch was a warm reminder of the magic they'd found, and she knew that she'd never tire of loving this red-haired giant of a man who'd showed her such joy.

As for giving, she had her own plans. And she'd show him, if all went well, in just about nine months.

THE EDITOR'S CORNER

There is never a dull moment in our LOVESWEPT offices where we're forever discussing new ideas for the line. So, fair warning, get ready for the fruits of two of our brainstorms . . . which, of course, we hope you will love.

First, expect a fabulous *visual* surprise next month. We are going to reflect the brilliance of our LOVESWEPT author's romances by adding *shimmer* to our covers. Our gorgeous new look features metallic ink frames around our cover illustrations. We've also had a calligrapher devote his talent to reworking the LOVESWEPT lettering into a lacy script and it will be embossed in white on the top metallic border of the books. Each month has a color of its own. (Look for gleaming blue next month . . . for glimmering rosy red the following month.) So what will set apart the books in a given month? Well, the author's name, the book's title, and a tiny decorative border around the art panel will have its own special color. Just beautiful. We've worked long and hard on our new look, and we're popping with prideful enthusiasm for it. Special thanks go to our creative and tireless art director, Marva Martin.

Around here we believe that resting on laurels must be boring (could it also be painful?). And, like most women, all of us LOVESWEPT ladies, authors and editors, are out to prove something as time goes by—namely, *the older we get . . . the better we get . . . in every way!*

Our exciting news has taken so much space that I'm afraid I can give only brief descriptions of the wonderful romances we have coming your way next month. However, I'm sure that just the names of the authors will whet your appetite for the terrific love stories we have in our bright new packages.

Delightful Kay Hooper has come up with a real treat— not just one, but many—the first of which you'll get to sample next month. Kay is writing a number of LOVE-SWEPTs that are based on fairy tales . . . but bringing
(continued)

their themes completely (and excitingly!) up to date. Next month, *Once Upon a Time . . .* **GOLDEN THREADS,** LOVESWEPT #348, tells the love story of Lara Mason who, like Rapunzel, was isolated in a lonely, alien life . . . until Devon Shane came along to help her solve the problems that had driven her into hiding. An absolutely unforgettable romance!

In a book that's as much snappy fun as its title, Doris Parmett gives us **SASSY,** LOVESWEPT #349. Supermodel Sassy Shaw thought she was headed for a peaceful vacation in Nevada, but rancher Luke Cassidy had other plans for his gorgeous guest. This is a real sizzler . . . with lots of guffaws thrown in. We think you'll love it.

The thrilling conclusion of The Cherokee Trilogy arrives from Deborah Smith next month with **KAT'S TALE,** LOVESWEPT #350. Kat Gallatin, whom you've met briefly in the first two of the Cherokee books, is unorthodox . . . to say the least. She's also adorable and heartwarming, a real heroine. That's what Nathan Chatham thinks, too, as he gets involved with the wildcat he wants to see turn kitten in his arms. A fabulous conclusion to this wonderful trio of books—a must read!

Tami Hoag tugs at your heart in **STRAIGHT FROM THE HEART,** LOVESWEPT #351. Jace Cooper, an injured baseball star, was back in town, and Rebecca Bradshaw was desperate to avoid him—an impossibility since she was assigned to be his physical therapist. In this sizzler Rebecca and Jace have to work out the problems of a wild past full of misunderstanding. **STRAIGHT FROM THE HEART** is a sensual and emotional delight from talented Tami.

Patt Bucheister gives us another real charmer in **ELU-SIVE GYPSY,** LOVESWEPT #352. Rachel Hyatt is a Justice of the Peace who married Thorn Canon's aunt to some stranger . . . and he's furious when he first encounters her. But not for long. She makes his blood boil (not his temper) and thoroughly enchants him with her

(continued)

off-beat way of looking at the world. Don't miss this marvelous love story!

THE WITCHING TIME, LOVESWEPT #353, by Fayrene Preston is delicious, a true dessert of a romance, so we saved it for the end of LOVESWEPT's September feast. Something strange was going on in Hilary, Virginia. Noah Braxton felt it the second he arrived in town. He knew it when he encountered a golden-haired, blue-eyed witch named Rhiannon York who cast a spell on him. With his quaint aunts, Rhiannon's extraordinary cat, and a mysterious secret in town, Noah finds his romance with the incredible Rhiannon gets unbelievably, but delightfully, complex. A true confection of a romance that you can relish, knowing it doesn't have a single calorie in it to add to your waistline.

We hope you will enjoy our present to you of our new look next month. We want you to be proud of being seen reading a LOVESWEPT in public, and we think you will be with these beautifully packaged romances. Our goal was to give you prettier and more discreet covers with a touch of elegance. Let us know if you think we succeeded.

With every good wish,

Carolyn Nichols

Carolyn Nichols
Editor
LOVESWEPT
Bantam Books
666 Fifth Avenue
New York, NY 10103